# THE SECRET OF THE 14TH ROOM

REBECCA HEMLOCK

# THE SECRET OF THE 14TH ROOM

Bluecap Publishing

*Beloved, let us love one another: for love is of God; and every one that loveth is born of God, and knoweth God.*

**1 John 4:7 -KJV**

# BOOKS BY REBECCA HEMLOCK

Arctic Mysteries series:

*Bitter Betrayal*

The Granton house series:

*The Secret of the 14th Room*

Bluecap Publishing
Ashland, KY 41102
bluecapbooks@gmail.com
bluecapbooks.com

First Printing, 2021

*To Paul, the love of my life.*

.

# PROLOGUE

The heart monitor beeped in the background as Albert Wilson held the hand of his dearest friend Dorothy Corbin, the lady that had been his neighbor for the last thirty-five years. He tried to ignore it, because he knew that it would stop at any time and there was nothing that could be done. Her closest friends, members of the Granton Historical Society, gathered around her bed to say goodbye to the precious gray-haired woman.

Although Albert was not a member of the society, he knew each of them very well. The hospital room felt very small, but Albert could not tell if it was because there were so many people there to pay their respects or because there were no windows to allow the sunshine in. Mrs. Frankson buried her face in the shoulder of the lady sitting next to her and began sobbing uncontrollably. It was becoming too much for Albert. He really wanted to leave the room, but Dorothy had asked him to remain in the room when she left this world. He kept asking himself how he was supposed to sit here and watch his friend die. But he stayed because he was a man of his word. He knew it was because she didn't want to die alone. With a heavy sigh, Albert wiped the tears from his eyes before they could make their way to his salt and pepper beard.

Dorothy had not only been a client of his at the firm, but she was also a dear friend to his family. Albert was glad that his sweet wife Nancy was not there. This would have been too much for her. He'd left her at home crying and hugging their daughter.

Dorothy Corbin was a no-nonsense woman who was not afraid to ask anyone for anything, and she always got what she wanted. Not because she was mean or pushy, but because she was well-liked, and everyone she knew felt like they owed her. Staying in the room when she drew her last breath was not the only task she'd asked of him. Difficult as it was, this was the easy task.

Soon the sniffles and blowing of noses nearly drowned out the sound of the heart monitor, up to the moment it stopped. The room fell silent for a few seconds, then erupted with loud wails. Albert stood, bowed his head, and said a quiet prayer. He paused a moment more, watching a slight smile form on her face and then left, imagining Dorothy grabbing the hand of an angel that would take her to heaven.

Levi Corbin shut his eyes tightly. The noise of the over-crowded train station was about to make his head explode. He couldn't wait to get settled on the train. Maybe he'd finally get some peace and quiet.

"ALL ABOARD!" the conductor shouted as the train hissed. The long line of people trailed the train tracks to the staircase leading to the inside of the station that was built snuggly into a hillside. Levi noted that it hadn't moved much in the last twenty-five minutes. He picked up his bag as the line finally began to move again. Levi huffed from the frustration of only taking about four steps.

He could see the conductor coming down the tracks toward him in a hurry. He could tell that something was wrong by the worrisome frown worn by the man. Levi reached out and grabbed the conductor by the arm, catching the man by surprise.

"Is everything alright? What's going on?" Levi asked, trying to not shout at the man over all the noise. The man jerked his arm away.

"You'll be boarding soon. We've just had a few maintenance issues. Just please be patient, sir," the man replied before continuing his mission. A few more minutes slowly passed, and Levi decided to slip the small book he was carrying back into his pocket. He couldn't read in all the noise anyway.

"I wish this stupid line would hurry up," said a voice just behind him. He turned to find a young girl that looked to be about fifteen or sixteen, clutching a bag tightly to her side. Her pink button-up blouse and designer blue jeans made her look about nineteen or twenty, but she had the face of a little girl. Levi figured she was trying to look older.

"I know, right? My knees are killing me from standing so long," Levi grumbled.

"I have a very important appointment that I'll be late for if we don't get moving," she stated. Levi felt as if he was talking to a child that was playing dress up.

"I'm sure it won't be much longer," he tried to reassure her. He was partially telling himself as well.

After about twenty minutes more, they finally made it to the boarding steps of the southbound train. Levi began to consider turning around and going home, because the reason he was getting on the train was becoming too much for him. He was about to break down crying from a broken heart in front of all these people, and that was the last thing he wanted to do.

Mustering his courage, he walked through the small doorway of the train car and sat in the first available seat. After coming this far already, there'd be no point in turning back now. He watched as the people piled aboard the train, scrambling to find a seat before the car was full.

Soon it became very loud inside the small car. Mothers tried to keep their children seated and entertained while dads were looking for places to stuff bags of all shapes and sizes into the overhead bins. Once every seat in the tiny car was full, the murmurs of people chatting with the person sitting next to them, whether they knew them or not, grew in volume. The air grew thick and humid due to a large number of bodies in such a small space.

Levi turned to look behind himself at the rest of the car to see what was keeping everyone from getting seated. The teenaged girl who'd stood behind him in line was settled in the seat directly behind him. She smiled when she noticed him looking at her.

"Sorry, I got used to looking at the back of your head," she jested. He smiled in response, then turned back around.

Further back, Levi could hear a husband and wife having an issue with two of their children that couldn't sit quietly together without fighting. He also heard a crying baby that was somewhere in the mix. The longer he sat there, the less the noise bothered him. He'd begun to retreat into his own mind until he couldn't hear anything but the hollow blackness inside. The emptiness he felt inside told him that nothing mattered anymore. He wanted to get to his destination quickly, but why? What would he find when he got there?

Pulling himself back to reality, he turned back around to see if he could spot the conductor, trying to ignore the young girl that smiled widely at him, clearly trying to get his attention.

The conductor on the other side of the car looked like he was going to have a nervous breakdown trying to get people's tickets checked off amidst the chaos. He called out multiple times for tickets, but no one seemed to pay any attention to him. Considering how far back the conductor was and how little progress he was making, it didn't look like he would get to Levi's ticket any time soon.

While Levi waited, he pulled out his brown leather wallet and opened it up. Inside was a picture of an older woman who looked to be in her early sixties, sitting on a bench with a beautiful lake spread out behind her. Sitting next to her was a boy that was about twelve.

Every time he looked at that picture, he could smell the crystal-clear lake waters and feel the warm summer breeze on his face. That used to be his happy place, their place. Their annual fishing trips would be something he'd remember forever. Levi leaned forward in his seat, resting his elbows on his knees, and studied the picture.

The boy had a big smile on his face, but to be honest, it was a wonder that he even knew how to smile after all he had been through. He had no parents, no home, and no one to love him and take care of him until that gray-haired lady showed up. That was the thing about the picture he loved most; the love he saw in her eyes. The love that he would never see or feel again. He'd grown up with his grandmother, Dorothy. She meant the world to him and now his world was gone.

Levi almost didn't notice the engine lurch forward and begin to huff and squeal as it struggled to pull the tons of weight behind it. There was no turning back now.

He was officially on his way back to the small town of Granton, Tennessee, right in the middle of the Smoky Mountains. It wasn't a bad place to live; he had just been so desperate to grow up and make a life for himself that the first opportunity he had to take a job in any town other than Granton, he took. The more he thought about it, the more the regret took his breath away.

He really should've called Dorothy more, but it was no use to think like that. She was the only person who'd made him feel loved, and he hadn't returned that love the way she deserved. He went back to see her a few times, but he'd fought so hard to get away from Granton in the past, that when he did visit, he didn't stay long. This time there wouldn't be anyone there waiting for him, even though he still felt that there always would be.

Levi folded up his wallet and put it away. Then he

pulled a piece of crumpled paper out of his pocket and read it for the hundredth time.

*Dear Mr. Corbin,*

*It is with a heavy heart that I inform you of the death of your maternal grandmother, Dorothy Corbin. Your presence has been requested by the deceased for the reading of her will on the 23rd day of September, 2010 at 4:30 pm. This will coincide with the distribution of her estate to her heirs.*

*Best Regards,*

*Wilson & Wilson, Attorneys at Law*

Levi ran his fingers through his hair, then folded the letter back up and stuffed it in his shirt pocket.

"I'm sorry, sir, but I have to ask, are you alright?" the voice of the girl behind him cut into his thoughts. Levi turned around once again to look at her. Her back was against the aisle arm of her chair, while her legs were crossed and propped up on the armrest of the seat next to her, her bag covering them.

"Yeah, I'm fine," he replied. The girl quickly grabbed her bag, got up and settled into the seat next to him.

"You really don't seem fine. Would you like to talk about it?" she asked. Levi felt that she was using the situation for some conversation instead of really caring about what was bothering him.

"I'm Bella," she continued, sticking her hand out.

"Levi," he replied, grabbing her tiny hand and giving

it a gentle shake. Clearly, Bella wasn't going to leave him alone until she got some sort of conversation out of him. He leaned back against the seat, trying to think of something to talk to her about.

"So, where are you headed?" he finally asked, giving in to the girl's eyes that pleaded for human interaction.

"Granton, Tennessee. I just got hired as a personal assistant. What about you?" she returned.

"Same place, but I'm going to a funeral."

"Oh? Whose?" Bella asked, with a sympathetic expression.

"My grandma's," he replied.

The enthusiasm to help him quickly transitioned into sadness. "Oh, I'm so sorry. Were you close?" she asked.

"We used to be."

When he didn't continue, Bella decided she would change the subject and fill the void between them herself. She began telling him about her parents and where she went to school.

"I'm not that close with my folks either," she added.

While her attitude was teen-ish, she was a genuinely sweet girl, and Levi wondered why she was traveling alone. Given her age, he was also curious about how she had managed to get hired as a personal assistant. Did she do the interview fully online? The moment she met her employer, they'd know she was underage. He didn't think she would be in town very long.

"I don't mean to pry, but how old are you, exactly?" Levi asked. Bella's eyes widened at his question.

"Age is just a number and shouldn't have any influence on judging someone's maturity," she replied.

"I'm sorry," he quickly apologized. Over the course of the next hour or so, he tried a few more times to slip it into the conversation but never got a straight answer. This seemed to be a secret she wasn't willing to give up, so he decided to change the subject.

"Where are you from?" he asked.

She stared at him for a moment. He could tell she was choosing her words wisely. "I'm from Ohio," she replied.

Levi smiled, trying not to show sarcastic surprise at her vague answer. They were in Ohio. Why didn't she want to share any personal details about herself? Levi mentally decided that it was none of his business, and he would stop trying to find out if she was a runaway. Still, he considered if he should tell her that her act was completely transparent or keep quiet and let her try to be a grownup. In the end, he decided to keep quiet.

The hours slowly ticked by, and it wasn't long before Bella became interested in something on her phone. Levi relished the quiet. He admitted that Bella helped him get through the urge to cry, but the emptiness remained—a cold darkness that kept telling him he would never be loved again. He went back to staring out the window, watching the world rush by.

As the six-hour trip came to a close, the train hissed and clanked once again as it slowed to a stop in an old, red-brick train station. Levi stood and stretched the stiff muscles in his back and shoulders. Bella stood up also, grabbed her bag, and shot out the door. A large pile of people pushed their way into the walkway while trying to exit, get their bags, and gather children all at the same time.

Levi grabbed his one duffle bag and exited as quickly as he could. Once he was back on solid ground, he found Bella standing there waiting for him.

"Oh, I thought you left," he said with surprise.

"I just wanted to get out of the car before we ended up being the last ones out," she replied, smiling shyly.

"Good thinking," he returned with a smile and a wink. The two walked through Granton Station and came to a busy street.

"Well, Bella, thank you for the pleasant company, and I wish you luck in your new job," Levi said, holding out his hand. She blushed, smiled widely, and shook it once.

"Thank you, too, and I'm sorry about your grandma," she said as her smile turned to sympathy once again.

"See you around," he replied, starting down the familiar street. As he walked, Levi closed his eyes and took a deep breath of the cool mountain air. It seemed to relax him a bit. He needed to relax before taking care of business and attending the funeral, which would be one of the hardest things he'd ever done.

But first, he had the meeting with the lawyer today. That was something he also wasn't looking forward to. He hoped he could meet with them before the reading of her will to ask a few questions. Who were the "heirs"? He figured if Grandma, of all people, had written a will, that he would be the one to get everything. Surely she didn't leave anything to Silas, did she?

Silas was his first cousin and the bane of Levi's existence. He had never treated Grandma with the respect she deserved, and he'd never even told her that he loved her. Levi and Silas never did get along, even though Grandma always tried and tried to help them become friends.

Levi's stomach began to rumble as he made his way toward the center of town. He figured he had time to grab a bite to eat and a cup of coffee before the meeting. He'd head to the old diner that was on Main Street. Grandma used to love that place. As he turned the corner toward Main, he thought about the last time Grandma had mentioned the relationship between him and Silas.

"If I could accomplish one thing in this life, it would be to see my two grandsons as best friends," she told him.

"That'll never happen, Grandma," he said flatly. He remembered seeing the pain his words brought her and wondering if she would cry or not. It was moments like that he really regretted. But it was hard to imagine himself ever getting along with Silas. They were so different.

Silas was the type of person that liked to flash a lot of money that he "couldn't say where it came from" and always had a new "girlfriend" with him anytime he came around.

Levi worked a steady job, barely making ends meet. There wasn't time for him to think about dating.

Lately, Levi saw Silas quite often. Silas didn't live in Columbus but came through town regularly. He knew that Silas never came by his money honestly, and Levi was often tempted to turn him in, except that would mean getting involved with Silas to prove his suspicions. And he'd rather be hit by a bus than spend any length of time that wasn't necessary with Silas.

Glancing around at his surroundings, Levi was struck with all the memories he had here. Granton was a historic town, named after General Grant himself, and its rich history was what drew in the tourism, which helped the town flourish.

Walking down the street of the two-hundred-year-old town, Levi took in the historical landmarks and sights that the town took pride in. The Civil War cannon, the old buildings, the statue of Grant that was erected in 1910. Every church, store, and even the houses looked the same as they did when he was a child.

The afternoon was warm but nice, and the breeze brought a graceful whisper from the trees. Levi drew in a deep breath until his nose was tickled with a touch of maple and coffee.

He glanced at his watch to double-check the time and quickened his pace. He still had about an hour and a half before he could meet with the attorney. Disappointment hit him when he saw that the diner was no longer there. In its place was a quaint coffee shop called Taylor-made Coffee. The storefront was decorated with pumpkins and fall garlands.

As he entered the shop, the smell of coffee grew stronger. It seemed to be a popular place, considering almost all of the tables were full. Levi approached the counter and scanned through the menu. The special of the day was half-off a caramel maple latte and a turkey and swiss sandwich on rye with a cup of vegetable soup, so that was what he chose. When the barista returned with his order, he took the tray of delicious smells to a little table in the corner.

As Levi sipped on his latte, he stared out the window at the little town he used to call home. He recalled when he was just an 8-year-old boy being brought to this tiny town to live with a lady he'd never met. He remembered how scared and fascinated he'd felt walking into his grandmother's huge Victorian home. The front of the house had enormous marble pillars—that were long overdue for some polish—and sun-faded black shutters covering the windows.

Roses of all colors and sizes were growing on either side of the big porch, being the first to greet anyone that would come to call. A black, Victorian fence about waist high surrounded the beautiful garden, protecting the roses from animals or anything else that was inconsiderate of Grandma's hard work.

He knew that the house was built just before the

Civil War, so Grandma's decor inside was mostly antiques and Civil War relics, which she thought was appropriate and complimented the house. You could hardly tell what kind of wallpaper she had up for all the things she had hanging on her walls. When his 8-year-old self walked through the front door for the first time, there was a huge plate of oatmeal cookies sitting on the coffee table waiting for him, but they came after several squeals and hugs.

"What a fine-looking young man you're turning into," she'd said, cupping his cheeks in her warm, wrinkled hands.

"Hi, Grandma," he said in almost a whisper. She stared into his face for a moment as a tear ran down her face.

"You look just like your mom," she said softly. Giving him one more hug, she told him how much she was going to love having him stay there with her, and she sounded like she really meant it. It was nothing like he'd imagined, which was more a frowning grandmother that insisted he call her by her first name, like he'd seen in the movies.

"Now, your room will be upstairs, first door on the left. You can go see it if you like, while I speak to this nice young lady," she'd told him. Grandma then turned her attention to the social worker and invited the stern-looking woman into the kitchen for a cup of coffee. Levi snatched up about six cookies then completely explored the upstairs and the yard, fascinated by all the history that the house contained.

Later that evening, after having his first meal in his new home, Grandma took Levi out on the big front porch and told him stories about how Ulysses S. Grant visited that very house during the Civil War. She also told him about when her grandmother (his great-great-grandmother) met General Grant in the flesh, and he gave her an amazing gift, but she never told or showed anyone what it was, except her. He'd begged her time and time again to tell him what the gift was, but she wouldn't.

"You'll find out later. All I can tell you is that seven plus seven equals fourteen," she always said.

"Grandma, I already know that," was always his reply. Levi remembered how fascinated he was by her stories. She was the reason he loved history so much and currently worked as a tour guide, teaching kids about American history.

It became a tradition for the two of them to sit on the porch after dinner, eating cookies and drinking lemonade while she told him story after story. Over time, he and Grandma became very close. He loved her more than anyone else. She was special to him, and she had so many funny little quirks that would make him smile, like how she had each room numbered.

The living room was room one, the kitchen room two, and so on. When Levi got a little older, he noticed that she began to forget which room was what number. At the age of fifteen, he went around the house and wrote the room numbers on the walls to help her remember. He then helped her rememorize the thirteen rooms. Although her odd behavior confused him sometimes, Levi made sure that he never made her feel inferior about her unusual habits.

While lost in his thoughts, he drifted back to the summer when Silas first came out to stay with her. From the moment Silas set foot in the house, he was trouble. Grandma made cookies for him and tried to give him a welcome, similar to what she gave Levi when he first came to stay with her. He never touched the cookies.

"Those look disgusting," he'd quipped. Levi knew he was just trying to hurt their grandmother. That seemed to be what he lived for. Every time Grandma mentioned General Grant and his connection to the house, Silas would call her a crazy old lady. When she wasn't around, he would bully Levi and pick on him mercilessly. Grandma knew about the bullying, but also knew that his parents sent him there during the summer just to get rid of him. Because of that, she always tried to make Silas feel wanted, but he never returned her kindness.

Levi looked down at his watch to check the time. It read 4:00 pm. The letter said he needed to be there at 4:30 pm. How had it gotten so late? He'd been so busy thinking about the past that he'd completely lost track of time. He quickly gulped down the rest of his latte and soup, dashed out the door and up the street, not realizing that he was being closely followed by someone else from the coffee shop.

CHAPTER

2

Levi walked up to a beautiful set of stone steps lead-ing into an interesting looking building with long, black shutters and a massive clock centered on the front. Levi took a look around to mentally compare it to the rest of the buildings in town. Most of them looked very simi-lar, with the same red brick, white pillars, black shutters, and perfectly landscaped lawns on every corner, but this building was unique. He wondered if the town looked this way back in the early 1800s when the area was first settled. Many of the streets were still paved with the original smooth, faded bricks.

He climbed the old stone stairs and stepped into the lobby where a middle-aged woman in business attire met him.

"Can I help you?" she smiled.

"Yes, I have an appointment. My name is Levi Corbin."

"Oh, yes, please have a seat. Ms. Wilson will be with

you in a minute," she said, pointing to an area with two chairs and a lamp in the corner. He looked around the waiting area, taking in the architecture and oil paintings of Civil War soldiers and animals. The decorator had great taste. Levi then spotted a candle on the receptionist's desk that was responsible for the touch of vanilla that hung in the air. It was a nice touch, making the room feel just a little cozier. Pulling a small black book out of his pocket, Levi sat in the chair as he was told and began writing.

*I walked down the sidewalk of this town again. In my mind, I could envision General Grant and his army slowly riding down the red brick street on horseback. Yes, this town is that old. I'm kind of happy to be home, but my heart is so heavy today. The weather seems to be sympathetic. It has just started to rain, seemingly coming out of nowhere, which is pretty common for this area. I hope that we can get things over with soon.*

"Fancy meeting you here," a voice said sarcastically from above where he sat. He knew exactly who it was without having to look up. It was Silas and his all too familiar smirk. Any happiness he felt from being home was immediately sucked out of him. Levi had hoped to meet with Grandma's lawyer alone before their appointment, but it looked like that wasn't going to happen now.

"So, you're writing in a diary now?" Silas scoffed.

Levi slapped his black book closed and pushed it back into his coat pocket. Silas had that look in his eye; the kind of look that said he had something up his sleeve, which may or may not be legal. Levi's anger turned to curiosity. Silas was definitely after something. Maybe putting up with him for a little while would let him know what it was.

"Mr. Corbin," called a young woman from the doorway across the room, causing both men to look. She had long chestnut hair and dark, deep-set, green eyes. Her cheekbones were high, and her mouth curved like she was biting the inside of her cheek. She looked from Silas to him, letting her eyes focus on his. Levi's heart began to flutter. She was nothing like what he expected. He tried to hide the fact that he found her very attractive.

Both Silas and Levi were headed in her direction when Silas shoved his way in front of Levi and went to grab the hand of the woman.

"Hello—"

"Have a seat, please!" she demanded, pulling her hand out of his. She gave Silas a disapproving look. Levi hoped it was over Silas' treatment of him.

Levi looked at his feet, trying to keep from laughing at Silas' blushing face. He guessed that Silas thought charming her was the way to get something from Grandma's estate. At this point, he couldn't imagine Silas getting anything. Levi and Silas both sat down in the chairs that were in front of the big oak desk.

"I am Abigail Wilson, and I am so sorry for your loss, gentlemen. This must be very difficult for you both. I knew Dorothy very well and she was a wonderful lady."

Levi stared at her for a moment. He didn't feel as bad

about not being here for his grandma now, knowing that she wasn't all alone.

"Thank you," he replied.

"Thanks for the touching remark, but can we please get to the will? That is the reason for this meeting, isn't it? I'm sure you have other business to attend to."

"Actually, no. This is my last meeting of the day, and the remark wasn't for you. I genuinely cared for Mrs. Corbin," Abigail replied, giving Silas a look that made him squirm and cough uncomfortably. Levi again tried to hide a smile. Finally, someone that wasn't afraid to stand up to Silas.

"Anyway, it isn't common practice to read a will before a funeral, but your grandmother requested that things be handled this way. Her will might be a bit different than what you're expecting," Abigail continued. She pulled a paper from an envelope and unfolded it. With a huff, Silas shifted loudly in his chair. Levi could see that Abigail's patience with Silas was growing very short. She shot him another look before reading:

*Boys,*

*Neither of you got along growing up in my house. You both were put in my care by the grace of God so that you would have a proper upbringing. I hoped that one day you'd do something great together. By Grant's Army, you will! My home is a historic treasure, and you BOTH can make something great of it and you'll work together doing it, or you get nothing. It's for your own good. Family is all we have and we gotta keep it close.*

*I love you both.*

*Love, Grandma*

Levi sat back in his chair, stunned. Abigail was right; the contents of the will were not at all what he was expecting. He'd thought for sure he'd get everything. Levi hated the thought of doing anything with Silas, much less something long term like this. However, if he disagreed to the terms of the will, who knew what Silas would do to Grandma's precious possessions. Levi didn't have the money to fight the will in court and wasn't sure he wanted to. To him, it would feel like he was going against his grandmother. However, he knew that Silas wouldn't pay any attention to anything he had to say about the house. He was used to being ignored and mistreated by the man.

Levi's mind was drawn back to another time when Silas had wronged him. Levi was ten, and Silas, who'd come out for the summer, talked Levi into helping him build a lemonade stand, promising they'd make a fortune together. Levi did most of the work on the stand, and when it was time to set it up, Silas had "caught a cold." On his own, Levi made twenty dollars from the lemonade stand. Not long after that, Silas went back to Chicago with his parents, and Levi suspected with the twenty dollars hidden in his suitcase. That was the only logical explanation for the money's disappearance. After that, Levi had promised himself that he wasn't going to be Silas's money-making workhorse ever again. That promise still stood today. Levi glanced at Silas, battling the old feelings he felt after discovering his money was missing.

"Well, that's it, then. You will share the estate, and I have been appointed to look in on you once a month to make sure that you are both involved in its upkeep," Abigail stated.

Levi rubbed his temple. "And if one of us isn't involved?"

"Then that person loses all rights to the estate and Dorothy's personal property."

Silas leaned forward in his chair. "What if neither of us takes care of it?"

"Then the house will be turned over to the Granton Historical Society. Dorothy was a part of that group for years. She loved it." Abigail slapped shut the briefcase that sat on a small table next to her.

"I never knew she was part of a historical society," Levi stated with a quizzical frown.

"I'm sure you didn't. I don't recall seeing either one of you around Dorothy at all," Abigail replied. Levi wanted to protest that remark but couldn't. Levi was ashamed at the realization that the last time he'd been back was about six years ago, and he hadn't asked many questions about Grandma or her life.

"Well, gentlemen, it's getting to be closing time, and I think we've covered everything. I assume that I will see you both at the funeral tomorrow?" she asked, standing to her feet.

"Yes, of course," Levi replied.

"Wouldn't miss it," Silas said, looking Abigail in the eye. She seemed unfazed by his attempts to intimidate her.

"Good evening, then," she said, taking her briefcase in hand.

Levi, with Silas close behind, walked out before Abigail so she could lock the office door.

"See ya," Levi said, waving to her over his shoulder. Abigail smiled in reply before starting down the sidewalk and disappearing around the corner.

"Oh, she likes me," Silas said, pulling his cell phone from his pocket. Levi didn't even look at him as Silas called for someone to come and pick him up. It wasn't long before a black car pulled up to the sidewalk where they stood. Levi'd started to head back toward the coffee shop when he heard a familiar voice.

"Hi, Mr. Corbin." Levi turned around to see Bella, the teenager from the train, stepping out of the backseat of the car.

"Hello there, sweetheart," Silas said, sliding his arm around her. Levi stood in shock for a moment. Silas had to be blind not to see that Bella was clearly a minor. Levi knew that Silas was often with the wrong kind of woman but never thought he'd go for a child. Silas had never seemed like the pedophile type. Levi walked over and pulled Bella away from Silas, not realizing she hadn't noticed him standing there.

"You don't want to work for this guy, Bella," Levi said in a low tone. She smiled when she noticed who it was that was pulling on her arm.

"Oh, hi, Levi! Why not?" she inquired, frowning in confusion.

"He's not a nice guy," Levi said urgently.

"Yes, he is. Plus, he's paying me a lot of money."

"I'll thank you to leave my employees alone," Silas cut in.

"I don't care. I'm telling you—" Levi said, grabbing her by the arm.

"Look, you're not in charge of me. I can take care of myself," she said, pulling away from Levi. Silas smiled victoriously at him and slid into the car.

Levi couldn't believe what he was seeing. He watched in horror as Bella climbed in after Silas and stood open-mouthed as they drove away.

He needed to meet with Ms. Wilson about this. Technically, Silas wasn't doing anything illegal....yet, but maybe Ms. Wilson could give him some legal advice as to what he should do. He feared for Bella's safety and wanted to keep her as far away from Silas as he could.

CHAPTER

3

Abigail drove home that evening, wishing people like Silas Corbin would fall off the face of the earth. Creepy guys like that reminded her too much of her Uncle Ray. She shivered when he came to mind. Uncle Ray was a smooth-talking person with a pushy personality, just like Silas, which was why her mom, Nancy, was pregnant with Abigail when she met his brother Albert.

Ever since Abigail found out that Albert wasn't her biological father, she had a whole new level of respect for him. It took a special man to fall in love with a pregnant woman and be willing to raise a child that wasn't "really his." But that didn't stop Uncle Ray from popping up here and there to start trouble. Abigail had been sure he'd always be around to haunt them until he suddenly died when she was in her twenties. Still, every once in a while someone would come into her life that reminded her of him.

She remembered the gratification she felt when Uncle Ray found out that she was going to law school to join her father's law firm.

He'd always tried to hold it over her head that she wasn't really Albert's daughter. Abigail made the decision to join the firm to bring justice to women in situations similar to her mom's and women like Dorothy Corbin. She couldn't help but suspect that Silas might take advantage of the legacy she'd left for him and Levi. She would not let that happen. Abigail shivered in an attempt to shake off the menacing thought of Silas trying to grab her hand in the office earlier.

She understood that Silas and Levi had difficult childhoods, too, but didn't understand how they could just rush off and leave Dorothy alone in her senior years. Abigail remembered the day in the supermarket when Dorothy told Nancy, Abigail's mother, that her young grandson was orphaned and would be coming to live with her soon. Abigail was only a child herself but still remembered feeling sorry for that boy because he'd lost his mom and dad. Besides that one time, Abigail hadn't had much interaction with Dorothy until she graduated from law school ten years ago. It was then that Dorothy had asked her over for lunch to discuss planning a will. After that, Abigail had never wanted to leave her side.

It became a habit for Abigail to visit Dorothy almost every day. She would cook breakfast for her, take her grocery shopping, and would even give her a ride to church. Abigail's heart ached for her friend. She didn't want to think about that right now, but the memory played out in her mind anyway.

The day she couldn't find her friend in the house. She looked everywhere; Abigail eventually found Dorothy lying on her stomach in the rose garden. She ran as fast as she could when she saw the motionless form on the ground. Tears stung her face and her lungs burned as she ran. When Abigail rolled Dorothy to her back, she found that the woman's consciousness was slowly returning.

"I'm alright, dear," she said, as Abigail gently pulled her to her feet and helped dust her dress off.

"Are you sure? Did you faint?" Abigail asked her, trying to hide the fact that she was crying.

"I felt a little dizzy and must have fallen," Dorothy replied, acting as if it was nothing, but Abigail could tell she didn't feel well.

From that day on, she was never the same. Dorothy had told Abigail that she never heard from Silas, but Levi called her as often as he could. She always spoke more highly of Levi than of Silas. By observing the two today, she now had a better understanding why. Abigail wasn't sure what to make of Levi. In the few minutes she'd observed him during their meeting, he seemed to be a better person than Silas, but he was quiet, and that made it difficult for her to discern what kind of man he really was.

As she pulled her car up the gravel driveway of her parents' home, she rolled down the window and let the cool mountain breeze brush against her face. She could see dark clouds gathering above her, flashing as they filled with lighting. She knew she needed to hurry if she was going to get inside before it rained.

Her car sputtered, bumping up and down as the gravel crunched under her tires. She parked her car in front of the A-framed farmhouse with massive windows. It had been her home for the last thirty-two years, and at this point in her life, she had a hard time seeing herself living anywhere else.

As she opened her car door and stepped out, she glanced in the direction of the Corbin house, which could barely be seen through the trees. It was a big, beautiful old place, and she was honored to be the legal protector of it. She sighed and grabbed her bags and quickly ducked inside as big drops of rain pelted her head.

*****

The next day, after Dorothy's funeral, Levi walked along the old road in the direction of his childhood home. He'd walked more since he'd been in town than he had in a long time. His aching feet really made him regret not getting a rental car yet. He imagined himself in a shiny new car, driving the streets of his hometown. In his dream, Abigail appeared in the passenger seat. He knew he liked her, but would she actually go out with him? He would need to ask Abigail to drive him to the rental car lot this afternoon.

As he walked, his mind went back to the beautiful memorial service that the Granton Historical Society had held for his sweet grandmother. The body that laid in the mahogany casket looked nothing like her, but he'd always heard that people looked different at funerals. She had been surrounded by beautiful flower arrangements, and near the casket was a bulletin board covered in a collage of pictures depicting Dorothy's life

There were also a few photos with him standing beside her, even that photo he carried in his wallet of one of the times they went fishing. That was from the time he caught his first large-mouth bass. Of course, Silas was there at the funeral and made sure to put on a big show in front of everyone that attended. He sat in the front row, right in front of Abigail, occasionally sniffling and rubbing his eyes. Levi didn't know what he expected to gain by the performance. Abigail looked uncomfortable every time Silas glanced at her.

He could feel the stares of the people that sat behind him, burning holes in the back of his head. They all must hate him and Silas for leaving her to die alone.

Levi stopped walking for a moment to pull out his wallet once again and open it to the fishing photo of him and his grandma, trying to take his mind off the embarrassment he felt. As he stared at the photo, something flashed in his mind. Shoot! He inwardly kicked himself for forgetting to talk to Abigail about Bella. He would have to make himself remember to call her a little later when he was settled in Grandma's house.

Levi went back to walking, determining that he had about a half a mile left till he made it to Grandma's. He kicked some pebbles down the road as he let his mind rest on Abigail.

She had sat across the aisle from him at the funeral and might have been peeking over at him once or twice. He wasn't sure. She was a professional-looking woman and quite beautiful. She not only acted tough, but she looked tough. He wondered if many men had asked her out and if they lived to see the next sunrise. He wondered if he should try his luck. He might, but he would have to do it when Silas was not around.

Part of him felt guilty for thinking about romance just after leaving the funeral of someone he used to be very close to—someone he loved very much—but the feeling he had in the pit of his stomach said it was ok to feel this way right now. He'd dated a few times since living in Columbus, but each girl seemed to want a quick fling. He wanted to find "the one." He wanted a family, and maybe even children someday. Mostly, he wanted to be loved.

The familiar smell of roses from his grandmother's garden filled his nose. He'd made the two-mile walk in less time than he'd figured. Several cars sitting in the driveway of his grandmother's home drew a concerned look to his face, the furrow in his brow deepening when he saw a man standing near the cars with his hands clenched behind his back. Levi walked up behind him. He spotted the black car that he'd seen Silas and Bella climb into the day before.

"It didn't take you long to start something. What's going on?" Levi scoffed.

The man turned. "Hello, Levi. If I'd known you were coming here, I would have offered you a ride," Silas said, holding back a chuckle.

"You could've asked," Levi retorted, knowing Silas' remark was simply to point out the fact that he was on foot.

"Anyway, this valuable estate is ours, worth a lot of money, and I intend on using it for just that," Silas stated.

"And how do you think you're going to do that?" Levi inquired.

"By selling it, of course," Silas answered.

Levi stood staring at him for a moment in disbelief. He could almost see the dollar signs popping out of Silas' eyes.

"I really should have expected this from you. She's not even cold in her grave!" Levi ground out. His guilt turned to rage as all thought of Abigail dissolved from his mind.

"Yes, but she is in the grave, and I'm not wasting any time," Silas replied. Levi turned away from Silas. This was becoming too much for him. Silas continued explaining his plan without any regard for how it made Levi feel.

"Just a coat of paint here and there, plus a few thousand dollars, and this place could be a huge money-maker," he said, giving Levi the same smirk he'd given as a child when he knew no one could stop him from doing anything he wanted. Levi knew that Silas was cruel and greedy and would do anything for money, but this was a family heirloom. The house had been in their family for more than a century.

"Just what kind of renovations are you planning to do besides painting?" Levi asked.

"Just leave the planning to me," Silas demanded. Levi knew this was exactly the opposite of what was read to them in the will the day before. Without another word, he walked up the huge steps and into the house. If Silas wasn't going to tell him what he planned to do to the house, then he'd find out for himself.

As Levi walked through the door, he stood in the entrance to the living room just off the foyer. There stood three men taking measurements in the large, dusty living room and making large X's on the walls with blue and orange spray paint.

"Whoa, wait just a minute! What do you think you're doing?!" Levi cried, holding up his hands to stop them. The men turned around to see what was interrupting their work. The bigger of the three men spoke up and approached him.

"Our job. We are going to take down this wall. Who are you?"

"I am the co-owner of this house, and I am to agree to any changes that are made. I certainly don't agree with this," Levi stated, as he turned to go back outside but found Silas already standing in the doorway behind him.

"Look, Levi, we are getting ready to put this old place to good use," Silas huffed. He closed the door behind him and continued to stand in front of it.

"Just sign this paper and take this check for $50,000. You can head back to wherever you came from, and you won't have to give it a second thought," Silas said, placing a pile of papers on the coffee table.

"You didn't hear anything Ms. Wilson said yesterday, did you? If I sign those papers, we both lose it," Levi barked.

Silas calmly held up a hand to stop him from continuing. "I've already thought of that. You can come here now and then, and I'll stay here and keep an eye on things. When she shows up, I'll tell her you called and approved everything, and she'll never know," Silas explained.

"No, you can't just buy me out. I grew up here, and I'm not gonna let you destroy Grandma's house," Levi shouted as he stuck his finger in Silas' face as it twisted into anger.

"Look, I plan to make some serious money from this, so some updates are needed to do that," Silas replied as one of the men that was measuring interrupted him.

"Sir, you want this wall knocked down, too?" They had moved around the room, making notes and scribbles on the walls, marking the demolition that they were going to do. Levi needed to think of something quick if he was going to save the house. He didn't have the money to make Silas a counteroffer. He wished that Grandma would have just left the house to him. Silas wasn't even letting him grieve before trying to take what was left of Grandma and her legacy.

"Can't you wait a bit before you do this? We buried her today. This is pure disrespect."

"I'm not wasting any time. Are you going to take my offer or not?" Silas growled.

"I'm not. She meant nothing to you! Why do you even care?" Levi shouted.

"Because you were her favorite!! The way I see it, you got her love and attention, I should get the house!!" Silas shouted back. Levi stood silent for a moment, shocked. Then his shock turned to rage. He was tempted to drive his fist into Silas' jaw right then and there, but he couldn't do anything to protect the house if he was in jail, so instead, he turned away from Silas and walked down the hall to where Grandmother's room was.

He slammed the door behind him, hearing Silas shout, "Just sign the—" as the door shut. Levi plopped down on the comfy, plush little bench that sat at the foot of Grandma's bed. A cloud of dust surrounded him.

"You must not have sat here very often," Levi spoke to the open air as if his grandmother could still hear him.

This room was not as musty as the living room, and he assumed it was because this was where she spent most of her time during the last weeks of her life. Levi began looking around the room. He hadn't been here in ages. It was like stepping back in time.

The walls were lined with oak shelves that stretched from ceiling to floor, mostly filled with history and antique books. Reading had been her favorite pastime. He stood up and walked over to her large, beautiful, old bookshelf that was located by the bedside and began to look through the titles on the shelf. How it must have felt to her to run her fingers through the spines, choosing a book. It was more to her than picking a random book to read. She treated each of these books like her children. It was the side of the bed that she slept on. She'd slept on the right side of the bed for as long as he could remember, so she could see out the window into the back yard.

As he scanned the shelf, one book caught his eye. A book with an interesting symbol on its spine. A golden eagle with its wings widely spread. It looked like a seal of some sort. Levi pulled it out and opened it to a page that had been marked. There he read about how Ulysses S. Grant gave Virginia Corbin, who'd lived in this very house, something very important. He gave her his Congressional gold medal a year before his death in 1885. Levi ran his fingers through his hair in disbelief.

Finally, Levi knew what the secret his grandma had kept was. It felt as if a small piece of his life had finally fallen into place. This story, and all the other stories surrounding it, all made sense now. Levi almost didn't know how to feel. Happy because he finally knew? Or sad because he couldn't share this with his grandmother? He wondered what Virginia Corbin's reaction was when such a special gift was given to her. Where was it now?

So, his great-great grandmother's name was Virginia Corbin. Levi only now realized he had never known the name of the woman he'd heard so much about throughout his life. Grandma Dorothy always just referred to her as ol' Grandma Corbin. Levi hadn't thought about it before, but if her name was Corbin, then she would have to be on his grandfather's side, not his grandmother's.

Levi flipped through a few pages of the diary-like book until he came to information about their family tree. There it read: Samuel Lincoln Corbin married Dorothy Ann Corbin. "So, Grandma's maiden name was also Corbin," he muttered to himself. He continued to read.

From what he could gather, Dorothy Corbin married her third cousin on her father's side, which wasn't uncommon when Grandma was a young girl. He flipped through a few more pages of the old book, then came to a page that had Ulysses S. Grant's family tree. There he skimmed through the names: Father, Mother, Brother, Brother, Brother, Sister- Virginia Paine Grant Corbin.

*Wait, what?* Levi thought to himself.

There it was, in black and white. *No way, this can't be!* But... it all added up with Grandma's stories. Why hadn't Grandma told anyone? His great-great-great uncle was

Ulysses S. Grant. This changed everything in Levi's mind about the house and the stories. Levi had always felt like he was a nobody, but his history now said otherwise. His grandmother was hiding a huge family secret that was a valuable part of U.S. history. This added to the story of General Grant and the Civil War.

The secret gift that Grandma had hidden was Grant's Congressional gold medal. He'd wanted to know that for as long as he could remember, and now that he knew, a warmth of pride filled his chest at his newfound history.

*No wonder Grandma was so obsessed with the Civil War,* he thought to himself.

This was a significant time, not only in the country's history but also in his family's history. Levi had to find a way to stop Silas from what he was planning to do. The only problem was, how? He couldn't afford to buy his half from Silas; working for the Ohio historical group giving tours didn't pay much.

There must be something he could do...

*Wait, the medal! If I could find it, I could prove without a doubt just how valuable the house was. Then no one would let Silas tear this old place apart.*

Quickly, he started flipping through the pages of the book he'd found to find any kind of clue as to where the precious artifact was but found nothing. Levi knew he couldn't let Silas in on this. There was no telling what the man would do with this information. He sat for a moment trying to figure out some way to stall Silas from doing anything else to the house. Levi knew he had to get this news to Abigail. She would know what he could legally do to protect the house from Silas.

He stood to his feet and untucked his shirt. Silas hadn't said anything about wanting to sell the valuable antiques, but Levi didn't want to take that chance.

Levi stuffed the book down into the waistband of his pants and tucked his shirt back inagain. He then slipped his jacket on and adjusted the hidden book so that it would be invisible to onlookers.

Levi looked around his grandmother's room once more to make sure he didn't leave anything out of place, then went back out into the hallway and tried not to look suspicious. Silas immediately noticed him, took a step toward him, and was about to speak when Levi shot up a hand to stop him.

"I don't want to talk about it anymore. I'm not selling my half," Levi said, trying to sound as if he was still very upset. He pushed past Silas, walked out the front door, and started the long walk back to town. Levi hurried as quickly as he could, almost sprinting to get out of view.

*Wow, that really worked!* He was afraid that he made it look too obvious that he was hiding something, but Silas never stopped him. Levi laughed a bit to himself. That was the first time that Silas had ever backed off from him.

Abigail sat in her office rubbing her temples in an attempt to get rid of a headache caused by a difficult client when Levi walked in.

"Hello, Mr. Corbin. How can I help you?" Abigail asked, trying to sound better than she felt. She gestured for him to sit in the chair across from her desk.

"I found something a bit odd in Grandma's bedroom today. Something I'm not sure you've dealt with before, but I didn't know who else to go to," Levi began.

"I don't know, I've dealt with some pretty bizarre things," Abigail replied. Before Levi sat down, he pulled the book from its hiding place in his shirt. Abigail's expression changed from her pleasant business face to confusion.

Levi began to tell the amazing tale of his great-great grandmother's visitor and how the visit deemed the house a more significant historical site than originally thought. Then he told her about his family background and his relation to U.S. Grant. She was fascinated by the information and the book that was lying on the desk between them.

Next, he told her of Grant's solid gold medal and his hunch that it was hidden somewhere on the property. Finally, he told her of Silas's plan to completely remodel the house and destroy the historical treasure.

"She went through so much to make sure the house was preserved," Levi finished. Abigail sat, listening closely through her splitting headache, trying to keep the details in order so that they would make sense when he finished.

"Well, you got me. This is beyond bizarre news, Mr. Corbin," she said, looking at the outer cover of the beautiful, old book.

"I didn't know how to handle the news myself. Um, can I say something off the record?" Levi quickly added.

"We didn't have an appointment, Mr. Corbin, so technically this whole meeting is off the record."

"I don't feel like Silas can be trusted with this information. Money means more than heritage to him. That's why I came to you instead of going to him," Levi explained.

Abigail was really good at reading people, but she was having a hard time reading Levi Corbin. He seemed genuine; she hoped he was telling the truth.

"Well, first of all," Abigail began, "because you legally own half of the house, Silas cannot do anything without your input. If he does, he's going against the stipulations of the will. He will lose his half, and it'll all go to you. Did you tell him verbally that you disapproved of the changes?"

"Yes, I did," Levi replied.

"Then if even one hole is made in the drywall, he's out. Furthermore, Silas has a right to know about this, but personally, I agree with you. So, I won't tell you what to do about it."

Abigail picked up the phone and spoke to her secretary, telling her to make an appointment with Silas to meet the next day.

When Abigail hung the phone up, Levi looked like he had something burning on his mind.

"Have you seen my cousin's assistant?" he asked.

Abigail paused for a moment, looking as though she was trying to keep from saying something about it.

"Yes, I have," she replied, her mood instantly turning from pleasant to fuming.

Levi leaned back in his chair as though he expected those words could bite him.

"Well, she is younger than she says. I'm worried for her safety around Silas," Levi explained.

Abigail stopped him before he could continue.

"We had the same thought then. Don't worry, I have already contacted the local police, and they are checking up on her for me as a personal favor." At that moment, the phone rang. "That was my secretary. The meeting with Silas is at noon, meet me here ten minutes early,"

Abigail told him. She had no idea why Silas brought out these feelings in her. She couldn't stand him and didn't have a good enough reason why. They had no evidence that Silas would hurt the girl. It was all just a hunch.

"I would also like to know how I can get the books analyzed to check their authenticity," Levi added.

"I feel like that should wait until after the medal is found," Abigail explained. She felt that Levi wanted the books checked for more reasons than money. He didn't seem like the type of guy with dollar signs in his eyes. She hoped she wasn't wrong.

*****

The following day, Levi stood on the steps of Abigail's office building just as he had two days ago. It was 11:30 am and he had been sitting outside of Abigail's office for forty-five minutes. He was a bit nervous about the meeting that was about to take place. He and Abigail had formed a plan to learn some details about Bella, but there was no guarantee it was going to work.

He couldn't remember anything helpful that she might have told him when they were on the train, even though Bella had opened up to Levi a bit and seemed drawn to him. She seemed to feel that they were "friends." He intended to use that to his advantage while Abigail kept Silas busy with legal details about Grandma's house and his renovation plans. He should've asked Bella where she was staying in town—being so young, she would probably appreciate a friend checking on her now and then—but he'd been too worried about his own problems.

He checked his watch to see that only a few moments had passed and wondered what time Abigail usually showed up for work.

*Why did I arrive so early? I'm making myself way too obvious.*

He thought he could catch her before their meeting and try to get to know her a bit, but now he regretted the idea.

"Oh, you're early!" Abigail announced, startling him.

Levi looked up from his watch to see Abigail staring curiously at him, holding a steaming cup of coffee. He wasn't sure what to say. Levi couldn't admit that he was nervous about talking to Bella, nor could he admit that he'd hoped to catch Abigail outside of her office to ask her to grab some coffee with him before Silas arrived. She seemed to have read his mind, because she turned back the way she'd come, then motioned for him to follow her.

"Come with me. If I'd have known that you were already here, I would have brought you a coffee, too," she said.

"That's alright," Levi replied.

"We still have time to grab you a cup. The greatest coffee shop in the world is just around the corner. We can probably get you a cup and be back before Silas shows up," Abigail said.

Levi smiled, forgetting about his nerves and the meeting with Silas.

As they walked, Abigail pointed and told him all about each building that they passed. She told him about each person that currently owned them; some names he recognized and some he didn't. She then told him a story from her past that connected her with each location. Some were hilarious while others were heartwarming. Levi was happy that she was letting her guard down around him. Abigail seemed to enjoy talking about the town. He could tell it meant a lot to her. Just as she was finishing up her story about the Granton Bank, they turned the corner and saw the huge sign that said "Taylormade Coffee."

"I came here the day before yesterday. Their coffee's pretty great. Unusual name, though," Levi told her.

"Taylor owns the shop. It's kind of a play on words," Abigail explained.

"That makes more sense," Levi replied, giving a nod. He held the door for her as they stepped inside the coffee shop, and Levi ordered a black, dark roast coffee.

By the time the two got back to Abigail's office, it was noon, and Silas was sitting inside, impatiently waiting for them. Abigail seemed embarrassed by the fact that they'd walked in together. As Levi watched Silas' expression change, he realized that the two of them together looked unprofessional on Abigail's part and just plain bad on his. He'd never do the things that Silas had done to get his way, but that was exactly what it looked like now.

Silas spoke with venom-laced words. "No wonder you didn't take the money. I didn't realize you used those methods of bribery, but guess what? I have some lawyers of my own that will shred the old woman's will to bits, leaving you with nothing."

Silas stormed out and slammed the door behind him. Total dread filled Levi as he turned to Abigail, realizing that she must not have told Silas that Levi was going to be present, which meant that his showing up with her looked even worse than he'd first thought. He felt that he'd just ruined her reputation and would also lose every part of Grandma's legacy to Silas. He was just about to apologize to Abigail when she sent an elbow into his ribs and gestured toward the bathroom. Bella was walking out with her cell phone in her hand.

She stopped dead in her tracks as she read something on the tiny screen. She looked up from her phone directly at Levi and Abigail. Levi immediately knew that Silas was texting her. He also knew that this ruined any chance they had of getting Bella away from Silas before anything happened to her. She stuffed her phone into her pocket, hurried past them, and bolted out the door. Levi and Abigail hurried after her.

"Bella!" Abigail called out, but Bella ignored her and quickly slid into the back seat of Silas' car. Levi watched them drive away once again, this time feeling more helpless than before.

Silas' frustration grew as the car hit the center of town. He ran his fingers through his jet-black hair, wondering how he was going to top Levi's unexpected move. Silas racked his brain, trying to figure out a way to remove Levi from Grandma's will without revealing his secret; that he couldn't afford to take the case to court. He couldn't really afford much of anything at the moment.

Silas had always liked to live above his means and knew it would catch up to him someday, but now was a bad time for that.

His biggest money issue was with the person whose phone call he'd been avoiding for the last few weeks. Jerry Delgado, a major loan shark in New York he did business with before working as an assistant to a very rich old man.

After playing the sweet, small-town boy for him, Silas had quickly gained his trust. It wasn't long before he was given the authority to write his own paychecks. That was exactly where Silas had wanted to be. He could give himself bonuses and raises anytime he wanted, and he took full advantage of his position. The old man never knew or suspected a thing until one day about six months ago. The man's daughter discovered one of the check stubs and told her father, but by that time, Silas was long gone. He had enough money to make it on his own for a while, as long as Delgado didn't catch up with him. But now, all his resources were drained, and he was in serious trouble. What he had in his bank account was it.

He was sinking every cent into Grandma's house, and he couldn't let this big break pass because of the sudden appearance of a guy that he'd hated since he was a kid. Grandma's house was worth a fortune, and he had no intention of sharing it with anyone. He knew that Levi would never help him financially, nor would he agree to go along with his plans. He just needed to be gotten rid of.

The lawyer was an unexpected hiccup in his plan, but after calling in a favor, she would no longer be a problem.

"Bella, sweetheart, what's the best place to eat in this crummy town?" Silas asked. Bella quickly whipped out her phone.

"How does Lamar's sound?" Bella asked.

Silas moaned, immediately recognizing the name of Levi's first high school job. "Fine. Fine!" he snapped, then explained how to get there to his driver. Bella quickly called and reserved their table.

Once they arrived at the restaurant, Silas wrinkled his nose at the familiar scent of garlic and fish. He hated garlic and fish because of this place. Levi would always come home from work smelling like garlic and fish, despite swearing that he wasn't near anything like that. The diner-like interior was filled with booths and tables, with a massive fish tank in the center of the room and a doorway in the back wall that led to an outdoor seating area. After the waitress took their drink orders, Silas figured he better check his bank account again just to be sure he could pay for this meal. He pulled out his phone and went online to check his account statements. He felt his heart drop to his stomach when he read the statement.

"What's up? Something the matter?" Bella asked.

"Nothing at all," he lied. The statement read that he had $52 in his bank account. He was supposed to have $52,000. That had to be a mistake. Silas knew that neither he nor his driver, Clayton, had made that withdrawal. *Someone took it, but who?* Things were not making sense. *It couldn't have been Delgado, could it?* Then he noticed that Bella was wearing a necklace that looked expensive.

"Wow, Bella, that's a pretty neat looking necklace," he commented. Bella's face lit up, and she immediately began to babble on, listing all the things that she had bought in the last two days and all the sales she had found since she'd been in town.

"I think it's a bit strange that I have $50,000 withdrawn from my account this morning after I gave you my credit card to get us breakfast," Silas accused. The smile disappeared from Bella's face. Silas knew it was her. He jumped out of his seat and grabbed her by the arm, dragging her out of the booth.

"You stole my money!" he growled, shoving her toward the exit. Bella stammered as she tripped and hurried in front of him, avoiding his grasp. Once outside, he slapped her across the face, leaving a giant handprint.

"You stole my money!!" he yelled.

"No! No!" was all Bella managed to get out. He continued to slap her and punch her with a consistent rhythm, asking why she'd stolen from him. Silas had felt the hopes for a better life fading away, and now a greedy child was trying to run off with what he had left. He was going to teach her a lesson. Silas's rage overtook his mind, controlling his movements. His heart pounded, and he could feel the veins popping out of his forehead and neck. Silas felt like a bull charging at the red, bleeding face of Bella. Then everything momentarily went black.

Silas was jolted back to reality by a sharp dagger-like pain throughout his body. He heard the rattle of a police taser, and his body jumped and began to tremble as he fell to the ground. Silas felt his arms being pulled behind his back and heard the sound of handcuffs closing around his wrists. He moaned as his head spun in confusion. In the midst of it all, he caught a glimpse of Bella lying in a pool of blood.

*Did I do that?* he wondered. He had never intended to hurt her that badly. As he was being pushed into the police car, Silas noticed two figures standing across the street, watching as he was being taken away. He couldn't make out their faces, but they seemed happy.

*****

Levi rubbed his temple, trying to plan out his next move on how to deal with Silas. The first plan he and Abigail had was a complete disaster. So, after the incident that morning at her office, they agreed to meet at Taylor's coffee shop to discuss their next step. He looked up from the steaming cup in his hand and felt his day get a little brighter when he saw her turn the corner. Abigail burst into the shop and walked up to his table.

"I have an idea!" she exclaimed.

"About Silas or Grandma's house?" Levi replied.

"Kind of about both," she said as she pulled up a chair and laid her bag on the floor next to it. "Why don't we focus on finding Grant's medal? If you think about it, that medal would solve all our problems. This historical find will get more people involved with the property, and Silas will have bigger problems than just a will if he tries to mess with the house then." She stared at him, waiting for a reply. Her big doe eyes made butterflies flutter around in his stomach.

"Well, it's worth a try," he said. She excitedly jumped up and grabbed her bag.

"Ok, you said that you found the book with the information about your family in your grandmother's bedroom. Maybe there is another book with clues in there. We should go take a look!" Abigail grabbed his hand and pulled him out the door of the cafe and to her car. For much of the trip back to Grandma's house, Abigail spoke about how much she'd loved being around Dorothy and about how she'd loved to sit with her when they attended church together.

Then came a moment as if Abigail had run out of words. She sighed and let silence settle between them for a moment. Sitting back in her seat, Abigail occasionally glanced out the window. Levi could see that her mind was deep inside memories of his grandmother.

"Your grandmother told me that God loved me more than even my mom and dad. As a kid, I couldn't fathom that because of how often my parents told me that they loved me. As I grew up, God's love became more real to me. I went through some hard times, and even though my parents were right there, I felt that only God knew my pain."

Levi listened intently to Abigail tell of her Uncle Ray and how his role in her life changed in her mid-teens. That was when she'd found out what he'd done to her mother that resulted in her pregnancy with Abigail. She

never claimed him as her father even though biologi-
cally he was. She'd simply thought he was an unpleasant
uncle.

"I will never refer to that man as my father, because he is the last man on earth worthy of that title,"
she said as she finished her tale about Ray Wilson, sighing as if she had gotten a huge weight off her chest. A
father. That was something Levi never had.

He'd always wanted a father. He remembered growing
jealous toward some of his friends when they would go
on father-son outings on Father's Day or when he heard
the term "my old man."

"How disrespectful!" his grandmother would say.
When he grew older, he too saw the disrespect in it, because they were too prideful to say "dad." Being raised
by his grandma had turned him into somewhat of an old
soul.

Realizing the painful route his thoughts had taken
him, Levi decided to change the subject and lighten the
mood. "Do you still go to church?" he asked.

"Oh yeah, and quite faithfully, too." She smiled. "Why
don't you come with me tomorrow? It'll be sort of like
old times, and I know that my parents will be happy to
meet you," she burst out.

Levi's face scrunched up with uncertainty. To cover
his feelings, he decided to tease her. "I don't know, you
think I'm ready to meet your parents. This is only like
our third date," he said jokingly.

"Not like that!" Abigail tried to hide the blush that

was quickly flooding her face. "My parents knew your grandma, and they know you're back in town. I thought—"

"I'm teasing. I'd be happy to go to church and meet your parents. I haven't been to church for a long time. I think Grandma would be happy to know that I went while I was in town," Levi said, smiling at her.

Stepping out of the car, Levi pulled out his key to the house and unlocked the door, holding it open for Abigail.

"Thanks," she said, stepping through the faded door. Levi watched her study the relics on the walls and stop where Silas' men had made markings. He didn't want their little mission to turn gloomy, so he tried to direct her away from it all.

"This way to Grandma's bedroom," he said, starting down the hall and entering the dust-free bedroom. Abigail followed, looking the room over thoroughly.

"Now here's what I'm thinking," Levi began. "Grandma loved riddles and creating unique reminders when she began realizing that her memory was fading. I think that's what the symbol on the spine of the book was."

"So, the next clue has to be in another book with a marking of some sort," Abigail finished for him.

"I think it's a good place to start," Levi replied with excitement.

Abigail nodded and immediately began to slowly scour the bookshelves, running her finger along the leathery spines. Levi turned to the bookshelf that stood behind him and began looking for anything mysterious. He looked through every shelf, climbing the little ladder and reading every title one by one.

"I've never known any house to have a library this massive in a bedroom," Abigail said, stepping back from the shelves for a moment to look at a higher shelf.

"Yeah, I personally think it's pretty cool. One of the Corbins was very sickly and couldn't get out of bed, so someone decided to give them a full library just a few steps away so that the person didn't go mad from the isolation. Grandma told me that story years ago, but I don't remember who exactly it was that was so sick."

Abigail's eyes widened at the story.

"It's amazing that you have so much of your family history preserved. I don't even know what my grandparents' names are," she admitted.

"That's funny. I was thinking about how amazing it is that you have parents that sound really nice and raised you to be a nice person," he replied.

"Hey, you may not have had a mom or dad, but your grandma didn't do such a bad job raising you," Abigail retorted. Levi smiled and blushed a little himself for a change, unsure of how to react to the compliment. He climbed down the ladder and patted his hip pockets, looking around the room for the next shelf to check. That was when he noticed her staring at him.

She stepped toward him, and he looked into her big brown eyes. Quickly, she leaned forward and kissed his lips softly. Levi looked at her a moment longer, then turned away and began looking through the books again without a word. She stood there, wondering what had just happened, then began to do the same.

"I'm not sure what I'm supposed to be looking for," she said, letting her fingers trace the titles. Levi didn't reply. It was as if he was frozen inside. He didn't know how to act or what to say, so he thought it best not to say anything to avoid sounding like an idiot.

He walked to the small shelf that was at Grandma's bedside, thinking that if he acted as if nothing had happened, then maybe the awkwardness would go away. Levi was scanning the titles on the very bottom shelf when he noticed an old book shoved halfway under the bookshelf. He pulled it out and read the title. *The Map.* He hadn't noticed it before and Levi didn't remember it being there the last time he was in this room.

"This looks like it could be something," he finally managed to say.

Levi began flipping through the pages, which were mostly blank. Nothing. Flipping back to the start, he noticed that on the inside of the cover there was a drawn diagram. He held the pages upright to get a better look at the image. Judging by the placement of the road and the porches, Levi could tell that it was a drawing of the first floor of the house. He flipped to the back cover and saw another diagram which looked a lot like the second floor. In the top corner of the second-floor diagram was the number fourteen.

"Fourteen. Does that mean anything to you?" Abigail said, looking over his shoulder.

"No," he said, still holding the book up.

"This is turning out to be a full-blown mystery," Abigail stated.

All his life, Levi thought he knew everything there was to know about this house. He thought he'd heard all the stories, but now it was as if he didn't know anything about the house at all. There was one more story that Grandma was trying to tell, and he was determined to hear it.

Levi sipped the last bit of his coffee as he heard tapping at the front door. He glanced at his watch. Who could be at the door at this hour on a Sunday? He'd stayed at Grandma's house overnight but never told anyone he would be here. Levi placed his coffee mug in the sink and grabbed his house keys from the countertop, dashing for the door. He opened it to find Abigail's smiling face. She was dressed in a navy-blue blouse that was tucked into a mustard yellow pencil skirt. Her brown high-heeled shoes made her feet look feminine and small. Her hair was loose around her shoulders.

"Oh, good! You're home. I was hoping you'd be here. I hope it's not a bother that I came," she said shyly.

"No, um, I just wasn't expecting you," he said, fumbling with the keys in his hand. Not only did he not expect her, but he also didn't expect her to look so beautiful.

"How about letting me drive you to church?" she asked, briefly studying his hands.

"Um, sure! I hadn't yet figured out how I was going to get there," Levi said, closing the front door behind him and locking it.

"So, I see that Silas gave you copies of the house keys," Abigail began.

"Nah, I stole his. I have no idea where he is, and he can come find me if he needs them," Levi replied. The two quickly marched toward her car and climbed in. She started the car and let the engine spit and sputter for a moment, then turned for the old country road. He wondered if he should even think about the kiss with her around. Levi had tossed and turned all night thinking about it, kicking himself, calling himself an idiot. No way was Abigail interested in a guy like him. The kiss couldn't be anything more than an accident.

"So, what kind of work do you do?" she asked him.

"I work for the Ohio Historical Group," Levi answered, trying to get his thoughts together.

He yawned, and before he was able to further explain, Abigail asked, "What do you do there?"

"I am a guide on the site tours. I pretty much show people around old houses."

"That's cool," she replied.

He realized that he probably sounded cross. He wanted to talk more during the car ride, to talk about the kiss even, but he was afraid that his exhaustion would make it all come out wrong. So, he decided that now was not the best time, and he should keep the conversation on a safe topic.

They rode a while in silence, and Levi noticed that her smile had faded. He was sure that he'd offended her with his tone. He broke the silence with the last resort question, hoping to bring the chipper expression back to her face. "What are you thinking about?" he asked, looking in her direction and using the opportunity to study her face once again.

"Not much," was all she said. He wished he was better at sparking a conversation. The rest of the car ride was silent. He turned and stared out his window, lost in thought. He wished that she would ask him more questions. *If only Grandma were here,* he kept thinking.

Levi thought about the time he took a girl to meet Grandma not long after high school. She was gorgeous, and he knew he wanted to marry her. Grandma told him that if she was really the one, then he needed to blind himself from her beauty and figure out what was on the inside before he made any hasty decisions. That wasn't what nineteen-year-old Levi wanted to hear, and it resulted in Levi saying things to Grandma that he still regretted. Still, Grandma forgave him and made him cookies after he caught the girl cheating on him with Silas. How he wished for her wisdom right now.

"This is the church," Abigail said, pointing to a white building up ahead.

"Hmm?" Levi mumbled, falling back into reality. She quickly stopped, jolting the two of them forward.

"Sorry, I don't know what's with this car today," she said, looking at the steering wheel as if it was at fault for the sudden stop.

"It's alright." He smiled at her, hoping to catch her gaze. His heart sank a bit when she climbed out of the car without another word. Levi quickly followed as she pressed the button on her keyring over her shoulder. Levi looked around, taking in the beauty of the white church with the tall white steeple. It looked the same as it did when he'd gone as a small boy, holding his grandmother's loving, feminine hand. Abigail walked straight-backed and proud, smiling and waving at everyone she passed. It was easy to see that this was her home.

Levi shoved his hands into his pockets, watching his feet as he approached the worship hall.

"Levi," someone called. He looked up to see Abigail waving him toward her direction. She was standing with a middle-aged man and woman. He went and stood with the small group, wearing the kindest smile he could muster.

"Levi, these are my parents, Albert and Nancy Wilson," Abigail explained. Albert stuck out a weathered hand and shook Levi's extended hand firmly.

"We remember you very well. So sorry about your grandmother," Albert said.

"Thank you," he replied.

"We would love for you to come to our house for dinner, Levi," Nancy stated.

"That's a great idea! If you're not busy, of course," Abigail agreed.

"We can talk about this afterward. We'd best get inside before the sermon starts without us," Albert cut in, herding the small group toward the doors.

"Do you attend church regularly, Levi?" Nancy asked, easing up beside him as they walked.

"Well, no," Levi muttered, a bit embarrassed. He was raised to attend church, but when he left town, he never went again. The sanctuary opened up to reveal a colorful stained-glass window on the back wall and a cozy row of seats just below it. The elevated seats were empty, yet the congregational seating was bursting at the seams. Levi followed closely behind the Wilsons, maneuvering through the narrow aisles while dodging men and women laughing loudly and chatting away with one another.

The Wilsons made their way to the front of the massive, carpeted sanctuary. The dark blue carpet and stained-glass windows were welcoming and demanded respect. The family, plus Levi, settled themselves in the third row back. After he sat for a moment, he noticed that Abigail was nowhere to be seen. He slowly scanned the room, searching for her face, but she had vanished.

"Where did Abigail go?" Levi asked Nancy.

"You'll see," she said with a grin as if she was holding in a secret. That answer confused him, but instead of asking further, he decided to remain quiet. A moment later, a stocky, middle-aged man approached the pulpit and spoke loudly, even though there was a microphone covering his mouth from Levi's view.

The minister began with a few points about showing kindness and love to everyone. The same love that Abigail told him of the previous morning. It made Levi feel good to know that such love existed. He'd never known such love except from his grandma.

"Jesus never fails," the man finished.

After the minister stepped away from the pulpit, twenty or thirty robed figures marched from hidden doorways and filled the large space of empty seats found just behind where the minister sat. Levi only saw one familiar, heart-shaped face. He met Abigail's gaze and gave her a look that said, *"Wow, I'm impressed."* She dropped her head and Levi knew she was either hiding a blush or trying to keep from blushing.

The choir began to sing an old hymn that brought back forgotten memories of a ten-year-old Levi holding his grandmother's hand. Levi suddenly remembered seeing a much younger Albert and Nancy standing in the oak pews with a young girl of about eight or nine in a green dress sitting next to them. She was staring at her shoes and looked as though she was pondering the great secrets of the world.

Levi was snapped back to the present by the booming voice of the minister.

"That's one of my favorite songs," he said. The minister placed his Bible in front of him and began to teach about the life of Jesus.

"My sermon is titled, the fourteenth generation, the generation of blessing." That number flashed through his mind and reminded him of the map of the house and the "14" written next to it. He thought about his grand-mother again, walking through each room of the house counting.

"Eleven, twelve, thirteen," her voice echoed inside his head. Was there a fourteenth room in the house?

"Levi? Are you alright?" Levi looked up and saw Abi-gail standing in front of him.

"Huh?" He looked around and saw that Albert and Nancy were also staring at him.

"I think he fell asleep," Abigail said to her parents with a giggle.

"No, I—" Levi started to defend himself.

"That's alright, it happens to the best of us," Albert said, gripping Levi's shoulder firmly.

Levi really wished there was something about the ser-mon he could remember to counter the accusation but couldn't. He thought it best not to bring it up again. So, instead he smiled and played along, hoping he could still make a good impression.

"Nancy and I were wondering if you would like to join us for dinner this evening if you don't have any-thing else planned?" Albert reextending the invitation his wife blurted out earlier reminded Levi that he never gave an answer.

"We won't take no for an answer," Nancy chimed in.

"I'd love to," Levi replied.

*****

Silas felt cold. His head pounded like it had been used as a punching bag for a dozen people. He rolled onto his side and curled up in a ball. His aching back was driving him crazy, and his legs were nearly numb. He quickly realized that sleeping on his side wasn't any better, so he leaned up and opened his eyes. He couldn't see very clearly, but he heard voices coming from the next room.

"Jonathan learned his lesson," someone said.

"Out on fifty-two," the voice continued.

"Fifty-two..." Silas muttered in a half-conscious blur. He shot up. The room began to spin as his memory of the horrible event returned. He'd never intended to kill Bella. Silas was on pins and needles about this whole thing with Levi, and he needed that money to buy Levi's half of the estate. Why did she have to steal from him?

*I never thought I would end up this way. Going to prison for murder.*

He could never catch a break. Levi seemed to have gotten all the luck in the family, even after being or-phaned. That was the one pleasure that he got: rubbing his parents in Levi's face. He used to feel like a jerk after-ward and would go off to be by himself for a while to get through the terrible feelings. Deep down, he really did feel sorry for his cousin. No one should lose their par-ents at such a young age. Now he wouldn't have to deal with the estate or Levi. He was going to be behind concrete walls for a long time. The room started to spin as Silas stood to his feet.

The icy, gray cell seemed to get smaller as the minutes passed. A toilet in the corner. A small shelf just within reach for the one book and one magazine that sat on it. A chair next to a small, uncomfortable cot with no blanket. This would be his life now. This place was hell, and prison would be no different. Silas paced the tiny box for a while, thinking about all the things in his life that he could've done differently.

He quickly got tired of thinking of his life and began counting the lines on the walls that someone made to show the number of days they were in the cell. Every few minutes, he would glance at the book and magazine and continue pacing. Silas hated to read, but he was about to make an exception before he went nuts.

*****

Lively conversation and laughter echoed from around the Wilson family dinner table. Other than the million questions about his life and his future plans, Levi couldn't remember the last time he had this much fun. The Wilsons seemed to be kind and loving parents, something Levi had always wanted. He'd been hoping for another chance to be alone with Abigail, but that didn't seem to matter as much right now.

They were treating him as if he'd been a friend of the family for years; although, he did notice that Abigail hadn't said very much since dinner started. He stole a glance at her and realized she looked uncomfortable. He quickly thought back over the conversation, trying to remember if he'd said anything that might have offended her. He couldn't think of anything.

"Abigail, that reminds me. I have something I wanna show you about the Sylvester case," Albert announced as he stood to his feet.

"Sure," she said, sounding as if she had no idea what he was talking about but didn't want to expose that fact. She slid back her chair and stood, disappearing into the dark hallway just off the dining room that led to the study. Since they were already treating him as a suitor, Levi figured he might as well try to score a few extra points.

"Mrs. Wilson, I can help you with the dishes if you like," he offered.

Her face lit up. "That would be great, thank you, and you can call me Nancy," she replied.

They quickly cleared the table and carried the stacks of dishes into the large kitchen. As they washed, rinsed, dried, and put them away, their conversation switched to local history. Nancy went on about local mysteries, but Levi's mind was focused on the brand-new dishwasher in the corner.

"Mrs. Wilson, how come we aren't using the dishwasher?"

"Oh, that was a gift from my husband a few years ago. It's nice to use during big holiday dinners when there are a lot of pans and mixing bowls, but this china is more than one-hundred-years-old. I can't trust that it will wash them with the fragile love that I do."

"I understand," Levi replied.

"Besides," Nancy continued, "all their years growing up, I loved looking out the window, watching my children play."

"How many children do you have?" Levi asked.

"Just Abigail and George." Nancy's expression switched to sadness at the mention of her son's name. "He died about eight years ago. He was trying to save his friend from joining a fraternity on his college campus and it got ugly. My son ended up giving his life to save two others." Nancy took the last dish from his hand and wiped it dry, gently placing it on top of a neat stack in the cupboard. She then untied her apron and took the apron that Levi had borrowed and hung them both back on the hooks.

"Abby must still be busy with my husband. I'll make some coffee, and we can continue our conversation on the porch." Nancy began preparing the Old Bunn coffee maker before Levi could argue. Soon the two were swaying back and forth on the cedar-scented swing. The evening was cool, and Levi wished it was Abigail sitting with him instead of Nancy, but he was glad for the company nonetheless.

"What were we talking about?" Nancy asked, kicking off the porch to make the swing sway harder.

"You were telling me about your son," Levi replied.

"Oh, yes, my George! He was a lot younger than Abigail. She had already finished college and had been working with her father's firm for a few years when he died. We never found out who was responsible, but it put a fire under Abigail's career," Nancy sighed.

"I remember Abigail as a kid. I remember her sitting in church during a service. She was wearing a green dress, I think." Levi re-imagined the scene in his mind.

"You have a good memory, Levi," she complimented. Before Levi could reply, a siren screamed its way up the Wilsons' driveway. Both Levi and Nancy's heads darted to see what was responsible for the noise. A Granton police car screeched to a stop and a tall, thick officer leaped out of the car.

"Sheriff Grady! Is something wrong?" Nancy inquired.

"Mr. Corbin?" the officer called as he quickly approached the porch. Levi and Nancy stood, and Levi nodded. "Your cousin, Silas Corbin, attacked someone this afternoon," Grady continued.

"What?" Levi questioned in disbelief. Silas was cruel, and by no means to be trusted, but Levi couldn't picture him as violent.

"Who did he attack? Are they alright?"

"He attacked his assistant at Lamar's around 2:30 pm. I'm not sure she's gonna make it," the officer's grim expression conveyed that he was trying to hold in anger.

"I just thought you should know. Nancy, we may need Albert's help with this case," the officer finished.

"I'll fetch him," Nancy replied, her shocked expression turning to sadness as she disappeared into the house.

Abigail's heart pounded so loudly against her ribs that she was sure her dad could hear it. Things were going so well. She'd brought Levi Corbin, the prodigal son of Granton, home for dinner. Levi had been the topic of many family meals since he'd moved away, with remarks like "leaving Dorothy alone," and "he'll regret it." Abigail figured her parents would be cordial to him and help him figure things out with the house, but if she thought it'd stop there, she was wrong.

Mom had talked most of the time, asking him where he was living now and if he planned to move back to Granton. It was enough badgering that Abigail had noticed Levi looking at her a couple of times with an expression on his face that said one thing: HELP.

Now, Dad had pulled her away at the least convenient time and left the poor guy alone with her mom. She knew Mom would probably take him out to the porch swing; that was her usual practice whenever Abigail had brought a boy home as a teenager. Although she knew why her dad had pulled her away, she felt that discussing a random case could've waited 'til a better time.

Albert paced behind the mahogany desk as he conveyed the details of the case to her. Somehow, that desk used to seem a lot bigger. As he droned on and on, she realized, for some reason, it felt more like a lecture than her touching base with a business partner. Abigail had sat in that same chair many times to receive well-deserved lectures from him when she was a teen. And she'd lost track of how many times her dad had paced behind the very same desk and told her that the decisions she made daily affected her future.

Once, when she was sixteen, she'd wanted to go to a birthday party that her entire class was going to, but Albert felt that she should stay home and study for the midterm math test that would take place the next day. Abigail received the highest score in the class and became eligible for a scholarship because of it. After that, she always took his advice and quickly learned that he was typically right.

That was a lesson her little brother George also learned at sixteen when he wanted to marry his seventeen-year-old girlfriend. Abigail's friend Patricia had called her while she was away at college and told her that she overheard the two talking about an elopement. She called their dad as fast as her fingers could dial, and he was able to stop them and talk them into waiting a few years for a proper wedding. They broke up a few months later, and George then saw just how wise their dad was. They were all thankful to God that they found out about it when they did.

"So that's what I'm thinking," her dad said, stopping right in front of her. Abigail stared at him with her mouth open, trying to come up with a good answer to hide the fact that she hadn't heard a word he'd said.

"Um, well, I think that's an interesting way to think about it, Dad," she babbled, hoping he would buy it.

"How so?" he asked. She was busted. Letting out a sigh, she confessed. "Alright, I didn't catch the last part," she mumbled.

"Abby, I don't think you caught the whole part." He laughed, giving her the same smile he'd always given her when she was a little girl.

"You were never a good liar, Abby. That's why I think you are excellent as an attorney. You're trustworthy, and that is a quality that is reassuring to our clients. I'm so glad you joined the firm."

"Dad, you're stalling. What's this about?" Abigail asked, readjusting herself in her seat.

"You know exactly what this is about. Your mom is checking this guy out."

"Dad, please, I'm not sixteen. I'm an adult, this is a client, and what makes you think I'm interested any-way?!"

"I don't care who it is. I can tell you really like this guy, and I want to know about him before I give my daughter away." Albert plopped in the chair behind the desk, propped his feet up on the stool, and folded his arms.

"Dad, it's not that serious. I just think he's nice," she said, feeling as if her dad could see right through her. She knew deep down that she would never have a shot with Levi. He would handle the affairs with the house and go back to wherever he came from, but that made her want to know exactly where he lived in Ohio.

At that moment, Levi and Nancy burst into the room. Nancy had tears rolling down her face, and Levi's face was unreadable.

"Abigail, Bella's in the hospital," Levi said.

"What happened?" Abigail asked, searching both their faces for some hint.

"Silas nearly beat her to death. She's in a coma. They arrested Silas. He was standing over her body with her blood on his knuckles," Levi answered.

Abigail took a minute to process what was going on. For a moment it was difficult to breathe. They were supposed to protect this girl and get her away from him.

Albert stood and began rummaging through his desk. "We will take care of this, Levi. Don't you worry."

"What's going to happen?" Levi asked Albert.

Albert stopped and looked Levi in the eye. "If Bella dies, heaven forbid, then he will be charged with murder, but if she improves, he will be charged with assault," Albert stated.

"I'll take care of Silas," he growled.

Albert interjected. "No, please leave him to me. You and Abby go to Bella and see how she is doing."

"He's right, Levi. You can't do anything about him. My dad can give him the legal advice that he is entitled to by law," Abigail added. She could see that Levi was having a difficult time controlling his feelings. She had no idea what he would do if he saw Silas right now. She thanked heaven that Levi was willing to listen to them.

\*\*\*\*\*

Silas paced the small jail cell like a caged cat. He panted, running his fingers through his hair. *What happened?* He had no memory of exactly what he'd done to Bella.

*Was I really so angry that I blacked out?*

Nothing like this had ever happened to him before. Silas had been taken away from the scene so fast that he didn't even know if he was facing murder charges or not. So many questions filled his mind, and not having answers made him even more anxious. He had to get control of himself and think clearly.

He sat on the floor of the cell, crossed-legged, and placed his palms on his knees. Silas had taken a few classes of yoga just to learn how to calm himself when he was on the brink of a panic attack. Taking a deep breath, he stiffened his back and held it for a moment.

"Is that what you do when you're scared?" a voice said from somewhere to the left of Silas.

Silas looked to see who it was. "Who are you?" he asked the shorter, stout man with a receding hairline and glasses.

"I'm Albert Wilson, Attorney at Law."

For a second, Silas was relieved. He stood and leaned against the cold steel bars that separated them. He would finally get some answers. He furrowed his brow in thought, trying to remember where he'd heard that name before.

"Wait, you're Abigail Wilson's father, aren't you?"

Albert admitted that he was and tried to further explain why he was there, but Silas held up his hand to stop him.

"This is just a ploy from Levi to get my half of the house."

"Levi didn't send me," Albert stated.

"I don't care who sent you. I don't want your help," Silas barked. He turned and walked to the back of the cell.

Albert stood silently for a moment. "Alright then. Do you need anything?" he finally asked.

"Just to see my driver," Silas said, without looking at him. When the room fell silent, Silas turned and saw that Albert was gone. The big-shot persona felt like it was pulling Silas downward as it dripped off him. He took a deep breath again, trying to calm himself down.

Silas plopped himself down on the cot that took up a large portion of the cell and dropped his head in his hands. He sat there for a moment, then placed his elbows on his knees for support. The feeling of utter hope-lessness weighed heavily on him, making it hard to breathe. Silas felt like he was drowning and everyone was watching him take his final breaths. Tears filled his eyes and fell, making little puddles in his hands.

*Will I ever find a way out of this?* He had dug himself in too deep this time. Silas considered calling in a favor from his lawyer to get him out of this murder charge, but then he would have to let Grandma's house go. He couldn't do that. That house was his last chance. It was his last valuable asset, and he needed to find a way to make some money from it, fast. It was also the last place that felt even remotely like home.

*****

Abigail clutched the steering wheel tightly, quietly staring down the winding road. Levi sat slumped in the passenger seat, rubbing his forehead with his index and middle fingers. Abigail was worried about Bella, but she was growing even more worried about Levi. She knew what Dorothy wanted to accomplish between the boys, and she had prayed with their grandmother every day that God would help unite them as their childhood should have.

"Family is everything! Good or bad," Dorothy would say. She had a lot to say about family. "You can change who your friends are, but you can't change your family. God knows what He's doing."

Abigail smiled at the memory of her old friend. Dorothy would know what to do if she were here right now. Each passing day seemed to push the boys further apart, and Abigail was starting to feel like she was failing Dorothy. She stole a glance at Levi. He now had his chin resting upon his knuckles, staring out the window. The country back road slowly became lined with shops and other small businesses. The leaves were starting to change in Granton from dark green to yellow and red, and neither of them had noticed. Abigail used the changing of the leaves to fill the silence.

"I can't believe fall is almost here," she said.

"Why would he do something like this?" Levi interjected, ignoring her comment. "He's always done what was best for himself, no matter who it affected, but I never would have thought he'd go as far as to beat up a teenage girl," he muttered.

Abigail thought it best to remain silent and let him get it out of his system.

But he didn't say anything after that. Abigail wished with all her heart that she had an answer for how to help Levi and Silas form some sort of relationship for Dorothy's sake. She had already disliked Silas for the kind of person he was, but now she disliked him even more for hurting Levi and Bella.

Granton hospital had cars lined up neatly on one side and a parking garage five stories high. On the other side was the emergency room with a small parking lot. Abigail navigated the car to the emergency side's parking lot, where she noticed that none of the cars were parked correctly. Each car sat partially over the clearly marked yellow lines.

Abigail understood why. She thought for a moment how she would react if she had to bring one of her parents here; she wouldn't care how she was parked either. The two walked the short distance to the emergency room. Abigail's chest tightened; she'd hated hospitals ever since George passed away. The waiting room was filled with people. There was a couple in the corner with a little girl. The mother was pale and had a bucket in her hand which Abigail assumed she'd vomited in. The woman's husband held her around her shoulders, supporting her because she looked too weak to sit up on her own.

A few feet away sat a middle-aged man in a wheelchair with one twisted leg elevated. Behind him was a nurse who sat behind a large desk. Abigail approached the desk with Levi at her heels. The nurse typed away on her computer then stared at the screen for a moment.

"Excuse me, ma'am," Abigail said, causing the woman to jerk her head to look at her. The woman's deep-set brown eyes intimidated Abigail, and she stumbled over her words. "We are here to see Bella...." She looked at Levi for her last name. Levi shrugged. It'd never occurred to Abigail that she would need the girl's last name until now, so Abigail resorted to descriptions.

"She's a teen with dark brown hair. The assault victim from Lamar's," she finished.

That seemed to be all the nurse needed. She typed a few things into her computer and stared at the screen for a moment. "Are you her family?" she asked. Levi and Abigail looked at each other then back at the nurse.

"Well, no, we're her friends," Abigail replied.

"I'm sorry, she is in intensive care, and if you aren't a blood relative..."

Abigail leaned over the desk and whispered to the woman. "Her family doesn't know she's here. We think she is a runaway, and we are trying to find out who her parents are."

The nurse looked unimpressed.

"I'm an attorney," Abigail finally added. The woman sighed and touched a few more keys on her keyboard.

"She is on the third floor in room 315D—"

"Thank you," Abigail blurted out before the woman could finish. She took off down the long hallway, looking for the first available elevator she could find.

Levi was beside himself with grief when he saw Bella. He'd known she must have been hurt badly to end up in the intensive care unit, but the state they found her in was far worse than he could've imagined. She was barely recognizable. Her face was swollen and purple from the severe bruising, and her hair was matted from the dried blood. Machines beeped and buzzed around her.

When Abigail saw her, she burst into tears and rushed to the girl's bedside. Levi followed and stood next to her, wrapping an arm around Abigail's shoulders.

"How could anyone be so cruel!?" she cried out, turning to bury her face in Levi's chest, which burned with hatred toward his cousin. Levi was asking himself the same thing. *How could he do this to another human being? To a child?* Levi vowed to personally see to it that Silas paid for it. He looked out the little window that gave the nurses station a view into the room. A few police officers were standing at the nurse's station talking with a short nurse. Levi almost didn't see her peeking over the countertop.

He did recognize one of the officers as the man that came to Abigail's house and told them of Bella's assault, though. The officer next to him was tall and thin, and the last one looked like he may have dyed his hair blonde. Levi left Abigail in Bella's room and approached the officers, jumping into the conversation.

"Is there anything I can do to help?" he asked, clasping his hands behind his back. The officers went silent for a moment. Levi gathered he must have taken them by surprise. The tall one spoke first.

"Who are you?"

"I'm Levi Corbin, Silas Corbin's cousin," Levi replied. "But I want nothing to do with him. I want to help this girl. I spoke to her a few days ago when I came into town. We came in on the same train."

The older officer pursed his lips in thought. Levi guessed that the man was deciding if he could be trusted or not. "We found an ID in the girl's wallet. Her name is Isabella Rodriguez, and she's from Columbus, Ohio."

"I knew she was from Ohio, but she wouldn't tell me where," Levi told him.

"Did you know she was a runaway?" the officer asked.

"I had no idea," Levi lied. He'd suspected her to be a runaway from the moment they'd met, but if he told the officer he knew that she was, they might think he was involved in this incident somehow. A pang of guilt hit

Levi. He inwardly beat himself up again for not getting involved earlier.

"We've contacted her parents. They're on their way," the officer finished. Levi felt a little relief in knowing that the girl wasn't going to be alone here. He looked back into the room where Bella was. Abigail was sitting at the bedside watching the girl. She wiped her eyes a few times and reached for a box of tissues that sat on the table next to the bed.

"Can you let us know if there's anything we can do to help the case?" Levi asked. The officer nodded a reply, and Levi left the group. He walked back into the windowed room where Abigail sat and placed a hand on her shoulder.

"Her last name is Rodriguez," Levi told her.

Abigail nodded.

"She's in a coma, Levi. They're saying that it doesn't look good for her right now because of all the brain damage," she said. Levi squeezed her shoulder.

"Her parents are on their way," he finally said. Abigail burst into tears again.

"I can't imagine how they must feel," she cried as Levi lifted her to her feet. He was fighting back tears himself, but he needed to be strong for Abigail. He squeezed her tightly as she leaned into him.

"We should go. There's nothing more we can do right now," Levi whispered to her. He grabbed her hand and led her back through the hospital and the parking lot to where the car was parked. Abigail pulled the keys from her purse and prepared to unlock the driver's side door, but Levi took the keys from her hand. She seemed to get his message; she didn't look up to driving. Without a word, she traded sides with him. Levi started the car and began the drive back to Abigail's house.

When they reached the house, only Nancy was there. She sat on the porch swing where she and Levi'd chatted just an hour or so earlier. Nancy placed a steamy cup of coffee on the porch railing and met them at the steps. Abigail told Nancy everything they learned and the condition that Bella was in.

"Oh, my Lord!" Nancy said, covering her mouth with her hand. Levi stood quietly behind Abigail, noticing that Nancy had changed her clothes. Instead of the knee-length dress with high heels she had on earlier, Nancy wore a red t-shirt and a denim skirt with a white paint stain around the hip area in the shape of a handprint. She looked as though she were about to start on some long project that would potentially ruin her clothes.

Levi waited until the conversation faded away before he asked about it.

"Nancy, I hope this doesn't sound rude, but were you about to work on something?" he asked, gesturing toward her clothes.

Nancy looked down at her clothes. "Oh, yes, I know I'm a mess. Albert had to go into town for something business-related, and I figured I'd continue working on the guest bedroom without him," she explained. Nancy shivered as a breeze began to blow.

"Would you two like some coffee?" Nancy asked, wrapping her arms around herself. Both Levi and Abigail nodded. Nancy disappeared into the kitchen, and Levi turned to Abigail, who seemed to be feeling a little better. She still had tear stains on her face, but she was breathing more deeply now.

"Your mom is a great lady," Levi stated softly. Abigail just nodded again.

It felt like just a few moments passed before Nancy returned with three steaming cups of coffee on a tray. She set them down on the coffee table and hurried back to the kitchen.

"Do you know the difference between a coffee table and a tea table?" Abigail asked.

Levi figured she was using the subject change as a way of helping herself calm down and be in a better mood. He shook his head. It was something he'd never thought about before.

"That's a tea table," she said, pointing to a tall end table that sat in the corner of the room. It had an antique vase on it and a family photo with a huge frame. "Tea tables are tall and often placed at the end of a sofa. Tea wasn't served on them, but they were set there during a conversation. People from the Victorian era were all about their beverages. Where to set them, and where to serve them," she finished. Levi smiled at her and she returned it with one of her own. He was half tempted to kiss her, but her mom came back into the room carrying small containers with cream and sugar in them.

"There we go," Nancy said, stepping back to admire the neat array that was set up. Then she sat down on a chair across from Levi and began chatting about the church service that they attended that morning and all the people he had met, giving him a brief history of each one. Levi couldn't remember the last time he was so relaxed. He felt happy for a change. A change he desperately needed.

*****

As Silas waited impatiently in his cell, he looked at the clock on the wall: 8:45 pm. His driver was supposed to be there fifteen minutes ago, and visiting hours were over at 9:00 pm.

*Strange, this isn't me at all.* Silas was growing impatient, because all he could do in the cell that kept him from going insane was pace. He now didn't feel like pacing and was sure that he was going to go insane anyway.

Suddenly, there was the creaking of a door opening, and Silas made a mad dash for the edge of the cell. He pressed his cheek against the bars to see who was coming. A uniformed figure came down the long hallway and opened his cell door with a clack and a bang.

"Your bail has been posted, Corbin," the officer said, scowling at him. Silas didn't reply. He walked out of the cell and waited for the officer to close the door, then followed him back down the hallway and through a door to a well-lit room. It felt so good to be free at last.

A long desk with several officers behind it cut the room in half. There was a man in the corner being frisked before presumably being taken back to where Silas had just come from. He pitied the man. Nothing was worse than jail.

In the back corner of the room stood Clayton, dressed in all black with a baseball cap on. Silas thought the outfit suited him, but knew Clayton only wore it to hide his identity.

"Hey, Silas," Clayton waved.

"Clayton, it's about time," Silas said, accepting the items that were taken away from him when he was arrested. Clayton stood waiting for Silas to approach him, but Silas pushed his way past and went straight for the doors and then to the car. He stood next to it, waiting for Clayton to catch up with him and unlock the doors.

"Silas, before we go, I think we should touch base on a few things," Clayton began, leaning on the hood of the car. Silas looked at him in surprise. Then a twinge of fear hit his stomach. "You know why I'm 'working' for you," Clayton said, using his fingers to make air quotes.

Silas dropped his head. He was so used to playing the big shot, telling Clayton what to do in front of everyone, that being reminded now and then that he wasn't actually in charge was a humbling experience for him.

"I got a call from New York, and the boss is getting tired of waiting for his money," Clayton finished.

THE SECRET OF THE 14TH ROOM

"Did you tell him that I'm doing the best I can?" Silas shot back at him.

"I told him you got yourself arrested for beating up a girl."

"Killing a girl is more like it." Silas sighed and placed his hand on his hip. That was the one aspect of this that he wasn't proud of. He hadn't meant to hurt her. Really, he probably should have given her a chance to explain what happened to the money he had left.

"The Boss thinks you're playing around and trying to make a run for it," Clayton's voice interrupted his thoughts.

Silas paused for a moment to think about what he should do next. He knew Levi wouldn't budge in selling him his share of Grandma's house. And he also knew he would lose his own share if he did anything to it without Levi's consent. It wasn't like Levi cared what happened to him anyway. All he cared about was the house.

Silas then had an idea. That house was everything to their grandma. She would've done anything to keep it from falling into disrepair, to the point that she must've had everything insured. Silas hadn't thought about the insurance.

If something were to happen to the house, then he and Levi would have to split the money, and he would be out of this mess. Clayton finally unlocked the car doors. Once inside, Silas began telling Clayton his great plan while the man drove them to the Granton Inn.

*****

As Levi was driving back to his grandma's house, he thought about the whirlwind of emotions and activity they had passed through. What started out as an evening to get to know Abigail and her family better, turned into a day in which everyone learned what Silas was capable of.

Levi rolled down the window of the rental car and took a deep breath of the crisp, chilly air. It reminded him of Abigail; she was so refreshing to him. Nothing like what he'd expected from an attorney. She was honest and fair in her work, and her faith and love of her family made him think of Grandma Dorothy.

He was coming up on the turn to go to the house but decided he would go back to town first. Levi hoped the grocery store was still open; he could use some drizzle corn and grape soda. The road grew dark and Levi turned the headlights on. The shadowy, secluded road to town took on an air of creepiness. He sped up to get into the lit up town.

When he got into town, it wasn't as lit up as he'd hoped. He wasn't used to the small-town way of closing up after 10 pm. Levi pulled into the grocery store parking lot, grateful to discover that it closed at midnight. After parking the car, he walked briskly into the store and found the items he'd come for. He was walking past the snack department when he saw someone that looked very familiar.

Someone who looked like Silas' driver was almost running through the store, grabbing items like a madman and throwing them into his shopping basket. Levi followed him for a bit, trying to remain unnoticed. After the driver had nearly filled his basket with various foods and toiletries, he went to check out. Levi waited until the frenzied man was gone to come out of the aisle that he was hiding in and check out himself.

*Strange*, Levi thought. He'd just exited the grocery store, giving a glance around the parking lot to see where the driver had parked Silas' car, when he caught sight of the man darting across the street.

Levi kept walking toward his car while watching the man load up his purchases and climb into his. Before the car sped off, Levi noticed the rear window had rolled down. A hand popped out of the car and waved at him. Silas.

That answered all the questions Levi had formed in the store. The driver had posted bail for Silas. In another time and place, he would've suspected Silas of being hundreds of miles away by morning to avoid court, but Silas wanted the house too much. What didn't make sense to Levi was that if Silas was staying in town for the house, he would still be made to appear in court and go to prison for what he did to Bella. Something didn't feel right, and Levi was going to find out what was going on.

\*\*\*\*\*

The next morning, Levi shot up in bed and gasped. The room spun, and his head felt like it weighed fifty pounds.

"Just a dream," he said to himself.

He'd been dreaming that Silas and his driver were villains that had taken over the town, and he and Abigail were trying to rescue Bella from their evil lair. It was odd to him how much the dream resembled real life.

Levi climbed out of bed and dressed. He felt like a kid again being in this room. It looked exactly as it did when he moved out. His childhood belongings lined the walls, and his posters were still up as well. He wasn't sure if grandma left his things this way because she missed him or because she was unable to change the room because of her health. It wasn't something he needed to think about right now. After he finished dressing, he went downstairs to find something for breakfast.

As Levi passed the living room, a twinge of horror hit him in the gut; the front door was open as wide as it could go. Levi was sure he'd locked the door when he came into the house last night. He hurried over to the door and looked outside. There wasn't anyone in sight, so he shut the door and locked it again. The only people that had keys other than him were Abigail and Silas. Levi ran back into the living room and picked up the phone. This had Silas written all over it. He would kill Silas if he found any of Grandma's things missing. Levi dialed 911 and waited.

"Good morning," said someone standing directly behind him. Levi froze in surprise. It was a woman's voice. He slowly turned, the phone to his ear, to see Abigail standing in the doorway leading to the kitchen. She had her hair pulled back into a ponytail and wore a bright purple t-shirt and navy-blue shorts.

"911, what's your emergency?" said a voice on the phone.

"Uh... nothing," Levi stuttered and slapped the old rotary handset down.

"Did you leave the front door open?" he asked. Abigail nodded.

"I was making you some breakfast and overcooked the bacon a bit. I opened the door to let out the smoke. I'm sorry if it seems a bit forward. I used to do this for your Grandma. I really missed it."

"No, no! It's alright. Thank you. Wow, I must have been so worked up over the door being open that I didn't even smell the bacon," Levi replied. "I was about to have Silas arrested again for breaking and entering." Abigail gave him a look that told him she didn't know he was out of jail.

"His driver must have posted bail for him," he explained. Abigail stood quietly for a moment.

"I looked outside and didn't see any cars before I closed the door. How did you get here?" he asked.

"You know I only live a few minutes away, right? I walked here."

"But that has to be at least a mile and a half!"

"It's really not," she said, crossing her arms as if challenging him. Then, abruptly, she changed the subject.

"You know, you actually can't have him arrested for breaking and entering here. This house is still half his," she added.

Levi hadn't thought about that.

"Anyway, I thought we could try and look for more clues today," Abigail said as she turned to go back into the kitchen. Levi followed her to find that not only had she made bacon, but also eggs, toast, pancakes, and coffee. His stomach started to growl at all the amazing smells.

They both ate quietly, giving occasional glances to one another. Levi liked the fact that he didn't have to eat breakfast alone.

"Do you like the pancakes?" Abigail finally broke the silence.

Levi nodded, covering his mouth while he chewed.

"They're your grandma's special recipe," she added.

"I thought I tasted vanilla extract in there," Levi muttered, trying to hold back the emotions that were swelling in his stomach.

"So, where do you think we should start looking for clues?" Abigail asked, picking up her plate. She stood to her feet and began clearing the table.

"I don't know," Levi replied. "I didn't expect you to

come here and cook breakfast for me. Thank you again," he said as he grabbed her hand before she could pick up any more dishes.

"I know. I used to come over here almost every day and make breakfast for Dorothy, though, so it's just kind of a habit for me now. I think she would appreciate me doing it for you, too."

Levi let her pull her hand out of his. He was embarrassed by his actions and was beginning to think that she was just being a friend to him because Grandma asked her to. If that was the case, Levi thought it would be best to avoid any more romantic situations in the future; he really didn't want to embarrass himself any further.

He stood to his feet, and without a word, went to the bedroom to get the books that they had found clues in. Levi was determined to keep the focus today on finding that medal. A few moments later, he came back into the kitchen with the books and laid them gently down on the now clean table, noticing that Abigail had prepared the dishes in the sink to be washed later. Seeing him come in, Abigail dried her hands on an old dish towel and tossed it on the counter.

"I think we should start by looking through my family history book again. I didn't get to go over the information very thoroughly because Silas was in the house," Levi explained as he started arranging the books.

"Sounds good to me," Abigail said, placing two cups of

coffee on the table. Levi flipped open the book and got a blast of dust in the face.

"Nothing like that old book smell," Abigail joked, fanning away the dust that flew into her face as well. Levi began reading aloud about the Corbin family coming to America in the early 1700s and how they had fought sickness, hunger, and poverty when they first arrived.

There were two Corbin brothers that had begun the trip. Originally, one had started a family in England, and the other had stayed at their childhood home in France. Both brothers wrote to each other about wanting the family to reunite and start a new life together in America, but in the end, only one brother made it. The surviving Corbin carried his brother in an oak casket to the place they had hoped they would grow old together.

"Oh my gosh. That's so sad," Abigail said, cutting into Levi's reading. He glanced at her for a moment to see if she had anything else to say. Then, he continued reading.

Apparently, the surviving brother built two houses on their homestead: one for his family and the other for his widowed sister-in-law and her children. The two families lived there for five generations.

Levi stopped reading for a moment to process the information. He had never heard this story before, and he couldn't wait to read more to see what other amazing family tales he would find.

*****

Silas sat in the back of the car watching the same Granton sights pass him by. He had memorized the town in the short while since he'd been back: The courthouse, the coffee shop, Wilson and Wilson Attorneys at Law, the grocery store, the gas station. The order was in reverse going back to the Granton Inn, but it was still the same old town. Silas and Clayton shared a room just big enough for two men with luggage. Clayton traveled with two suitcases and Silas traveled with four. It sometimes seemed weird to travel with so many bags, but they contained everything Silas owned. They reached the motel and went to their room without a word. Even though the scenery was monotonous, Silas was still grateful to be out of jail.

The two double beds in the room were the same as every other motel the two had stayed in before. The sink in the bathroom was a slanted stone trough with a twisting spout. Silas had seen similar sinks when he was in Texas for a short while a few years back.

"He's at the house," Clayton said from the front seat. Silas stared at him blankly for a moment. He hadn't realized they were already here. Silas slid to the edge of the back seat and peered over Clayton's shoulder. Levi's car was sitting in the driveway. Clearly he was staying there. That would make things a little more difficult.

"Take us back up the road a bit so we can figure this out," Silas waved his hand forward then plopped back in his seat. If Levi was staying there, then he would have to find another way to get into the house and find the support beams. According to Clayton, their demolition plan had to go forward no matter what.

"The house will burn today," Clayton told him. He seemed to be showing more of an interest in this than Silas figured he would, but Silas really didn't want a murder to happen at the same time.

*Should we trick Levi into a meeting with someone, or should we simply wait until he leaves?* They couldn't just walk into the house; Levi would definitely expect him to be up to no good.

Levi had never trusted him, not even when they were kids. Levi had called him a crook and a thief time and time again until Silas eventually began to believe he was one and stole the boy's first wallet at the age of twelve.

"We need to hide the car and sneak into the house," Silas said, thinking out loud.

"You know he's gonna go out with that lady lawyer at some point," Clayton replied.

Silas nodded at Clayton's remark. The two watched the house from a small gravel spot on the side of the road just around the corner from Grandma's house. Silas hoped that Levi didn't have to go to town for anything today, otherwise he would pass right by them.

Clayton pulled an old pair of binoculars from under his seat and started watching the house.

"What'd I tell you?" he said after several minutes of silence.

"What!" Silas quickly slid back forward to see what was going on.

"That lady lawyer is there with Levi. They're sitting at the table talking," Clayton told him, handing over the binoculars. Silas gazed through them to see Abigail sitting at the kitchen table next to Levi. They seemed to be reading something.

*Rats!* Silas thought. He needed the house empty so they could go through with their plan.

"What should we do?" Silas asked. Clayton looked at the clock that sat on the dashboard of the car.

"It's about thirty minutes 'til lunchtime. Let's see if they cook or go somewhere for lunch."

"Shouldn't we hide better just in case they go to town for lunch?" Silas asked. Clayton shook his head in reply.

He sat quietly for a moment.

*Am I really going to do this? That house is over a hundred years old, and despite the bad memories with Levi, it was my home.* He thought about Grandma. Maybe if he had been nicer to her he might have been her favorite instead of Levi. Silas had always felt like she loved him, but he'd also always felt second.

About an hour later, Silas was feeling cramped, like he was back in his jail cell. He wanted to go for a run in the woods or something, anything, to get out of this car. The leather seats were starting to get sticky from his sweat.

"I'm gonna get some air," he told Clayton. Silas

opened the door and was preparing to slide out when Clayton tossed him a ball cap.

"Better put this on first, so it'll be harder for anyone to recognize you," he explained. Silas did as he was told and walked a few feet into the woods. He could still see the car and Clayton in the front seat. Silas was half tempted to make a run for it; Clayton would never find him in these woods. He knew them all too well. But if Clayton returned to New York without money from Silas, they would kill him instead. Silas sat crossed legged on the ground and began playing with some twigs and vines. He had to be alone for a while to think about this and running wasn't going to help his situation.

THUD!!

Silas heard the sound of a car door slam and looked up just in time to see Clayton speed off. Silas jumped to his feet and ran to where the car had been parked, but all he could do was watch as Clayton drove past the house and disappeared down the road.

"What in the world!" he shouted. A few seconds later, another car came speeding down the road in his direction. Silas ducked back into the woods and watched the car go by. It was Levi's car. Clayton must have been right; Levi and Abigail were going to lunch. After Silas was sure they were out of sight, he stepped out of the woods.

He looked toward the direction of the house to see Clayton coming back down the road. The man pulled back into the spot where he was before and Silas climbed in. They drove down to the house and pulled into the driveway. Silas climbed out of the car.

"Get the car out of sight, just in case they come back and we're still here."

"On it," Clayton replied. Driving the car around the corner, Clayton parked it behind one of the large out-buildings.

Turning back to the task at hand, Silas unlocked the front door and stepped into the house. He could smell the remaining fragrance of bacon from the breakfast they must have had together.

"Let's go," Clayton said from behind him. Without a word, Silas turned and followed him up to the attic located at the end of the upstairs hallway behind a door that was smaller than the others. Clayton opened the door and let Silas squeeze his way in front of him. Clayton followed. Then, both walked up the tiny staircase to a large, open room. A musty smell hit them both in the face. A moth fluttered around the window and a cloud of dust hung in the air.

"Wow, this is bigger than an apartment!" Silas exclaimed as they reached the top.

"You've never been up here?" Clayton asked.

"We were never allowed," Silas explained without looking at Clayton. There was a tiny window close to the floor at the far end of the attic. Silas went to it, knelt down, and peered out of it. It gave a clear view of the driveway and front steps. "Convenient," he muttered to himself.

"What I'd like to know is how your grandmother was able to afford to keep this place this long," Clayton stated.

"That lady lawyer would know," Silas replied.

Clayton shrugged and set down the equipment he'd brought with him. "Now, let's get to work."

Abigail watched Levi slowly close the book. He had read some pretty amazing things about his family and what they went through, with both major triumphs and tragedies throughout their history. It seemed to be a lot for him to take in. When Abigail had first made the trip over here, she had worried that her reason for coming sounded a bit flimsy. She did love coming to cook breakfast for Dorothy and learned a lot from her, but her grandson was a whole new challenge.

She liked Levi a lot, but she knew that he would be going home after figuring things out with Dorothy's house and this business with the secret treasure. Abigail knew better than to let her feelings go as far as they had. She promised herself from now on she would suppress them and let them die; Abigail didn't need a heartbreak on top of losing a very dear friend.

Levi glanced at his watch. "It doesn't feel like we've

been reading this book for an hour and twenty-five minutes," he said.

Abigail furrowed her brow and looked at her watch as well. "Wow." She was a bit disappointed that the book hadn't offered any more clues so far, but there was no helping that now. Abigail needed to go to the office and do some work today, but first, she would have to go home and change. Working for her dad was a major plus in that department; Abigail only worked when he needed her to and got paid a lot for it.

"I have to go," she said, standing to her feet.

Levi stood as well. "Can I buy you lunch?" he blurted out.

Abigail paused. She knew better than to believe that spending this much time with him would help her kill her feelings for him.

"No, that's ok. I really need to go home and change. Dad needs me in the office today," she explained.

"You have to have lunch at some point. At least let me give you a ride home, so you don't have to walk it," Levi said with a shrug.

Abigail really didn't want to have to run back to her house, so she accepted. Levi gathered the two books and took them upstairs while Abigail grabbed her things and went to wait for him by the car. She stood for a moment looking at the side of the beautiful old house.

Not only was it the pillar of the Corbin family history, but it was also the historical pillar of the community. Dorothy had been working on making the house a historical landmark and had been in the process of going through the old records and organizing them. Abigail had hoped that her legacy would live on through the Corbin boys, but their feud had made that hope all but an impossibility.

After a few minutes, Levi stepped out of the house, turned and locked the door, then hopped down the steps. He unlocked the car for her and she climbed in. As soon as Abigail sat down, her phone rang. She answered it to find her dad on the line telling her that he needed her at the office immediately.

"Dad, I'm not dressed for the office."

"Come anyway," he said firmly.

Abigail didn't argue. She hung up the phone and turned to Levi. "My dad needs me in town now. He said it's urgent," she explained.

Levi pulled out of the driveway and started in the direction of town. As he was getting the car up to speed, a black car sped past him.

"Isn't that Silas' car?" Abigail said, turning to watch it dart around the curve.

"What would he be doing out here?" Levi peered into the rearview mirror.

"He didn't have Silas with him. The back seat was empty," she added. Abigail suspected Levi was rolling this information over in his mind.

"It looked like he drove right by the house, too," he said after a moment or two.

If he didn't have Silas and he didn't stop by the house

for any reason, then it was nothing they needed to worry about right now. Abigail pulled down the visor and looked at herself in the mirror.

*I wish I'd dressed properly.* Abigail thought to herself. Abigail was used to her dad doing this to her by now, but she was in her workout gear, and her hair resembled more of a bush.

She pulled her scrunchie out of her hair and started running her fingers through it, combing out the tangles. She mumbled to herself about how awful she looked. Levi reached behind her and grabbed something from the backseat.

"I have a brush here if you need it," he offered.

Abigail felt her eyes widen with surprise. "Oh my! Thank you! You wouldn't happen to have a size 8 dress back there as well, would you?" she joked.

Levi chuckled.

"Unfortunately not, but if I can help you in any other way, please let me know."

"I would like someone to each lunch with. But it'll be my treat instead," she said, inwardly aware of the situation. Levi sat silently. Abigail was sure that she'd offended him by offering to pay. She stared at him for a moment chewing on the inside of her cheek while waiting for his response.

"Abigail, there's something I think we should..." Levi began.

"You mean the kiss," Abigail stated, certain they were thinking about the same thing.

Levi let out a sigh. He opened his mouth to say something again, but Abigail thought it best if she said it. "It was nice, but I think we should be realistic. I don't think we can have a future together. Once you finish things here, you're going to return to your job and your home, and my place is here. I'm not the long-distance-relationship type," she explained.

After Abigail finished her little speech, Levi didn't say anything. He drove her to the office and stopped in the street right out front. Abigail stepped out and turned to thank Levi for the ride. Her heart felt heavy with worry. She knew not to pursue a relationship with him, but wanted him in her life. She was tempted to ask him where they now stood.

"What time will you be taking lunch?" he finally asked, interrupting her thought.

"Two in the afternoon," she replied. Levi nodded and took off. Abigail stood there for a moment and watched his car disappear. She was starting to think that maybe she'd made a mistake. Abigail had never meant to hurt him, but in her attempt to protect herself from being hurt, she'd done just that. There was nothing wrong with protecting herself though, right? If a person put their heart out there for every person they had feelings for, then there wouldn't be anything left to give to the person they married.

With a sigh, she turned and walked up the stairs, through the door, and into the waiting area. Sarah, the receptionist, looked at her with wide eyes, scanning her outfit. Abigail realized she never came to work like this before. It must be surprising for Sarah to see her this way.

"Your father is waiting for you in his office," she said urgently. Abigail hurried in and saw Albert sitting at his desk. He was leaned over, writing something on a random legal document. It was the same image she remembered from when she was a child and could barely see over his desk. Of course, he'd had a lot less gray in his hair then.

"What's going on, Dad?" she asked, holding her arms out to her sides dramatically. Albert showed no reaction to her presence but continued to write for a moment, stopping only for a split second to gesture toward the chair that sat on the other side of his desk.

This office was set up very similar to the office he had at home, except this one had newspaper clippings in frames hung on the walls and pictures of important clients that her father had represented since he'd begun his practice.

Abigail went to the mini fridge that was hidden behind a massive armchair, grabbed two sodas, and went to the seat that her father had sent her to. She remembered her father leaving treats in there for her to find when she was a teenager. Sometimes he would even have candy or ice cream bars in there, and they would share them while she told him about her day.

"I've made a decision," he finally announced to her. Abigail stared at him for a moment, letting her mind return to the present, and waiting to hear what he would say next. Based on his expression, she knew that she wasn't going to like what he had to say.

"I've decided to represent Silas Corbin in the assault case," Albert said.

Abigail paused to roll his words over in her mind. "Dad, you know this is a losing cause. Dozens of witnesses saw him do it, and he was bailed out of jail yesterday. We don't even know where he is now," she said. But with each point she made, her father simply nodded and interjected an "I know." Abigail shook her head to make sure she hadn't imagined what her father said.

"What made you decide to do this, Dad?" she asked.

Albert stood up from his red leather chair and began his "thoughtful attorney" pace. "Abby," he began. "Dorothy saw something special in both those boys, not just Levi. Don't get me wrong, Levi is a good guy, but Silas has never been given the same chances that Levi has. Levi grew up with the love and support of Dorothy; Silas grew up with parents that didn't care about him. Dorothy wasn't going to give up on him, though, and I don't think I should either."

Abigail was taken aback by what her father had said. She didn't want to admit it, because of the type of man that Silas had proven himself to be, but she knew he was right, as always.

"I guess whoever said that it is better to have both parents than no parents at all, was wrong," she muttered.

"Well, at least in this case," Albert joked.

Abigail smiled at his remark. "If you know this is going to be a losing cause, then why do you want to take it?" she asked.

Albert sat back down in his chair with a thud that almost caused him to spin the swiveling chair in a circle. "To show him the love of Jesus," he said.

That was all Abigail needed to hear. She was sorry she had asked after hearing that answer. She should've known better. Abigail thought about all the Bible verses she knew about "doing unto others," and "the least of these."

"You let me know your game plan, Dad," she said. "And I'm here for whatever you need to do."

"I think I can handle this case by myself," Albert explained. "I just wanted you to be aware of what I'm going to do." He returned to his writing, and Abigail knew that was her cue to leave him alone. She grabbed her can of soda and got up to leave.

"Was there anything else you needed from me today?" she asked, turning back to him. Albert grabbed the can of soda that she'd brought over for him and popped it open.

"Have a good time with Levi," he said, bringing a blush to her face.

\*\*\*\*\*

Levi decided to do some exploring while he waited for 2:00 pm. He turned his car down a little alley and discovered an interesting looking building in the middle of the next block. He slowly drove past it, checking out the architecture. Once it became difficult to see, Levi sped up and continued driving. He hadn't been down some of these streets since he was a little boy, but some of them held vague memories for him.

Levi rolled down his window to let the crisp air blow in his face. The leaves had turned gorgeous shades of orange, yellow, and red, and there was one tree at the corner of the block with perfect shades of red and orange that made it look like the tree was on fire. But as much as Levi tried to enjoy the beautiful scenery, he kept thinking about what Abigail had said earlier.

*"I don't think we can have a future together."*

Did she say that to let him down easy, or because she honestly didn't think it would work? Levi wasn't the type to give up on something so easily, though. Despite what she'd said, he felt that the kiss had meant something, and he was going to find out what. It might be hard to convince Abigail to let him try, though.

While he kept looking around the town, his phone rang. Levi picked it up, surprised to see that Abigail was calling him. He pressed the green button to answer the phone.

"Hello?"

"Hey, Levi, you wanna go ahead and get lunch?"

"It's only just now noon," he replied.

"Well, Dad and I finished up early," she said, sounding strange. Something must've happened between them.

Levi figured he'd better cooperate, just in case she needed comforting.

"I'll be there in a few moments to pick you up," he told her.

"Sounds good," she said, then hung up. He pulled into a parking spot, whipped the car around, and headed back in the direction of her office. He hoped he could find the way back. He took in every detail to remember if he'd passed it before.

When he finally made it back to the office, Levi noticed that Abigail was a few yards away from the entrance, walking down the sidewalk.

*She must have given up on me coming. Did it really take me that long to get back?* He pulled up next to where she was walking and rolled down the window.

"Hey, need a ride?" he quipped, trying to be funny. She smiled, ran to the passenger side, and climbed in.

"You ok?" he asked her.

"Yeah, where should we get lunch?" she replied flatly. Levi could see that she was avoiding any conversation about herself.

"Well, I was thinking we'd try Lamar's," Levi said, hoping to still try to pay for lunch.

"Sounds fine," was her only reply. The two rode along in silence once again, and Levi was getting tired of the awkwardness between them.

"Abigail, I feel like we are too good of friends to keep this up. I know I'm still new in your life, but clearly, there's something wrong, and I think you would feel a lot better if you told me," Levi said suddenly. Abigail looked at him in surprise. She didn't seem to expect that to come from him. He hadn't either, but if he was going to have a shot with her, then Levi needed to show her that he cared.

"You're not going to like it," she told him quietly.

"Try me." He smiled at her, hoping it would give her confidence in him.

"My dad has decided to represent Silas in court."

"Wait, what?" Levi's face showed a look of disbelief. He was so caught off guard by her remark that as he turned toward her, his foot abruptly bumped the break petal. Both of them were lurched forward.

"Are you trying to kill us?" Abigail burst out. Levi didn't mean to startle her but had to crack a smile at her reaction. She must've realized how she sounded because she smiled and covered her now blushing face. Trying to push past the embarrassing moment, she continued with their topic of conversation.

"He made the decision, knowing that it is a losing battle for him," Abigail continued.

"It's definitely a losing battle; there's no possible way to make any case for Silas. Except maybe one of insanity."

"Well, my dad thinks he should help Silas because of his friendship with Dorothy," Abigail explained.

"Did he tell you that?" Levi asked.

"No, but he didn't have to. I know my dad. He loved your grandmother like she was his own mother."

"How did he become so close to her?" Levi inquired.

"That's a story for another time," Abigail's tone told him not to ask any more questions, so he let silence settle between them.

When they reached the restaurant, the two entered and Levi took a long, slow look around. He remembered working here; it was his first job when he was in high school. Levi remembered thinking that he was some kind of big shot for landing a job at the nicest restaurant in town, but his first day was spent mostly cleaning up messes that he'd made from dropping dishes, plates, and trays. He looked across the table at Abigail, secretly letting his mind drift back to their kiss. That was when the hostess came up, forcing him to put those thoughts away.

She asked if it was just going to be the two of them, then grabbed two menus. Levi discovered with surprise that they still used the same menus as when he'd worked there.

They were led to a table by the window with a view of a gas station just across the little side street that ran by Lamar's.

"So, since you worked here, would you happen to know how Lamar's got its name?" Abigail asked.

"Oh my," Levi exclaimed, adjusting himself on the padded bench.

"You have to know. All the employees know," she insisted teasingly.

"So does all of Granton. They acted like it was a great

honor to know, but then I found out that it was common knowledge around here. I mean, it's local history, for Pete's sake," he groaned.

Abigail laughed. "How old were you when you started working here?" she asked, still smiling.

"Seventeen, and boy did I think I was a big deal. Everyone else in my class started out working for their parents or some farmer mucking stalls."

The waitress appeared at their table side with a small pad and paper. She took their drink orders, and Levi was a bit embarrassed that he hadn't picked up the menu yet. He could see that Abigail shared his embarrassment. They glanced at it and quickly ordered.

"I'm really surprised that this place is so empty today," the waitress said, taking the menus from them. Levi looked around. It looked regular to him. There was someone at every other table.

"Since that guy attacked that young girl here the other day, people can't seem to stay away. It's the biggest thing that's happened at this place," the waitress continued.

Both Abigail and Levi darted a look at her. Levi felt a flush of emotions flow through him. Abigail's face darkened.

"For your information, that girl is in the hospital in a coma," Abigail said coldly. "She is in critical condition. Someone was nearly beaten to death, and you act like it's some kind of sideshow gimmick."

The waitress was left speechless by Abigail's remarks.

She stood there for a moment, and Levi thought that maybe she was trying to find a way to apologize, but then the girl surprised him.

"I'll put this order right in for you," the waitress said, then walked away.

There wasn't any conversation after that. Levi'd hoped this lunch would feel more like a date, but now that was out of the question. Once again, Silas had ruined something for him. After they paid their bill and left, Abigail asked Levi to take her home. He wanted to ask her more questions about her dad representing Silas in the court case, but she didn't look like she wanted to answer his questions. He decided it would be better to wait and ask her later.

Levi almost felt like he was alone in the car due to the silence. He could tell that this case was having a real effect on Abigail, and he was growing worried for her. When they got back to her house, Levi walked her to the door. He was about to reassure her that everything was going to be alright, but before he could, Nancy asked if he wanted to come inside and have coffee.

Levi declined, feeling like he'd bothered them enough. "I really need to get back to the house and finish some work with Grandma's things," was the best excuse he could come up with. Nancy accepted the excuse and bid him good night. Abigail waved at him over Nancy's shoulder as she disappeared up the stairs inside the door.

That evening, Levi drove himself out to the river that

was about a quarter of a mile from Grandma's house. He thought about taking his fishing pole but felt it was better to just sit on the pier and take in some peace. The shadows of the pine trees that surrounded the lake made it difficult to see what was going on under them, which made it easy for small animals to hide and sneak to the river for a drink.

Levi sat in silence, remembering how Grandma told him about the Native Americans that used to live there. He let his mind run wild as the crickets sang. Levi could imagine three Cherokee canoes slowly paddling their way down the river. Each canoe holding about four men. He imagined the animal sounds they would use to signal each other. Slowly, the canoes turned and banked on the other side of the river and each man climbed out.

A few Cherokee women came out of the tree line and met the men with smiles and embraces, but one of the men yelled at a woman that approached him with her arms open for a hug. She seemed to trust him whole-heartedly, but he still struck her and she fell to the ground. Another Cherokee man attacked him, but the first one had picked up a weapon and began killing the others. When the murdering brave turned around to go back to the canoes, Levi could finally see his face. He looked just like Silas.

"This is a beautiful spot, isn't it?" a voice behind him interrupted his thoughts. Levi jumped and spun around to see Albert standing behind him in a flannel shirt and jeans, carrying a fishing pole and tackle box.

"Mr. Wilson, you spooked me," was all Levi managed to get out with his heart pounding out of control.

"I love this spot," Albert said, walking to the end of the pier. He set his fishing gear down and went back to grab a stump of wood that sat next to a tree just a few feet away from the pier.

"I can't tell you how many times people have snuck up behind me since I've been here," Levi stated, turning back around. He looked back across the river. No one was there. There were no canoes, no signs of any Cherokees.

Albert let out a loud belly laugh. "People from around here all know each other, so you can kind of predict where someone will be at what time," Albert explained. "Like, I spend Monday, Wednesday, and Friday evenings fishing," he continued.

Levi stood and was about to say goodnight when Albert waved a hand at him, motioning him to come to the end of the pier. Without a word, Levi followed. Albert placed the stump down and sat on it like a stool. Levi didn't know what to do at that point, so he sat on the pier cross-legged.

"My son George and I used to come down here together. Did Nancy tell you about George?" Albert asked.

Levi nodded.

"He was a good kid. He got into trouble now and then, but he needed to know that, even at his lowest, he could always count on family."

Levi had a difficult time understanding what Albert meant by that, so he did not comment.

Albert flicked his fishing pole and watched the bobber smack the water and bounce up and down as the water rippled. He sat quietly for a moment then turned his head to look at Levi. "Levi, I'm going to defend Silas in court," he told him.

Levi nodded his head, conveying that he already knew.

"Do you know why I've chosen to do this?" Albert asked.

"Not really," Levi answered.

Albert turned back and faced the river. He took a deep breath and closed his eyes, then exhaled and opened them again. Without looking back at Levi, he asked, "Did Dorothy ever tell you about the 'root of bitterness'?"

"Yeah, I think I remember her talking about something like that," Levi replied.

Albert began to explain to him about what the "root of bitterness" was and how it can affect a person by digging its roots deep inside someone's heart. He told Levi that the plant itself is ugly and will give a nasty attitude to the person it is affecting. "Like a poison," Albert explained.

Levi tried to hide the fact that he felt like he was in Sunday School. Albert continued to explain examples of the root of bitterness in the Bible and personal experiences that he'd had with it. It sounded a lot like how things were between Silas and himself, but unlike Albert, Levi he didn't know if he was strong enough to change.

After about an hour of talking, it was growing too dark for either of them to see anything. Albert began packing his things and carrying them back to his car.

"You just think about what I told you. The right thing to do isn't always the best decision," he said as he disappeared into the shadows.

*****

Silas sat on the bed in his motel room, thinking about what Clayton had told him regarding his phone call from New York. He was beginning to think that it was best for him to just give up and let them kill him. A year ago, Silas thought he would be safer in jail, until he heard that they had sent someone to prison to kill someone else. That was when he learned that you can't hide from these people, no matter where you go.

He played with a granola bar wrapper as Clayton flipped through channels in search of something good to watch. After a few moments of restlessness, Silas thought maybe a shower would help him feel better after everything he'd dealt with. He knew there weren't any windows in the shower, so he could go in there without Clayton worrying that he was going to make a run for it. Silas had tried to tell Clayton that he knew better than to run, but he'd yet to convince him.

When Silas stepped into the flow of hot water, he let out a heavy sigh. The steaming water seemed to wash away all of his problems, and it was just him there in solitude. After relaxing in the shower, Silas went back into the main room and decided to try and sleep.

He had spent a lot of time with Clayton, and whenever he felt like they were forming a real friendship, Clayton would receive a call from New York, reminding him of his job. But, no matter how Clayton treated him, the man was still the closest thing Silas had ever had to a friend.

There were times he thought that when he hit his big break, he and Clayton could go somewhere far away and be out of range of any danger, but he was too often reminded that he was just a job to Clayton.

After an hour or so of tossing and turning, Silas heard Clayton climb into the other bed. Tomorrow, the two would go to the house to see their handiwork. He wasn't sure why this had to be done with fire, but Clayton seemed to have a lot of opinions regarding the house lately. Silas felt like Clayton was hiding something from him, but he didn't know what or why.

Either way, the house would be burned to the ground. They had placed a strange-looking contraption in the attic that was set to strike a match and toss it into a pile of insulation, then set it to go off twelve hours after they left so there was no sign of them having been there. Silas tried to imagine how Levi would react when all that was left of the house was a pile of ash.

It was difficult to picture that house gone, but it would be better than Levi having it all to himself. Silas would collect half of the money and be rid of New York, Levi, Granton, and Clayton once and for all.

The next morning Abigail awoke feeling like a sloth. She had very little energy to speak of and figured it was the stress of the last week. It was difficult for her to make her way down the hallway to the bathroom, because she didn't have the desire to stand for very long. Abigail took a long, hot shower, hoping that would make her feel better, but it didn't; she still felt like crawling into bed and sleeping for the next few months. Even so, she forced herself to get dressed and begin her day.

Abigail went down the stairs, rubbing her face with her hands in an attempt to wake herself up more. Her parents were sitting at the kitchen table sipping cups of coffee.

"Morning," Abigail mumbled, helping herself to what was left in the coffee pot.

"You've nearly missed it, are you feeling alright?" her

mother chirped, giving her a look of concern and grabbing her hand.

"Yeah, I'm fine, just tired," Abigail replied. Nancy dropped her hand and stood up to feel her forehead.

"You may be coming down with something. I don't think you should be going out today," Nancy said with concern on her face. Abigail did feel like she was coming down with a cold, but she wanted to go see how Bella was doing and find out if the girl's parents had made it to town yet or not. Her mother's hand on her forehead felt like it weighed a thousand pounds.

"I'll be alright," she said, removing her mom's hand. Abigail then picked up her coffee cup and sat at the table to join her parents. "So, what'd I miss?" she asked, peeking over the cup as she took a big gulp.

"I was just telling your mom about last night. I met Levi out by the river. We had a nice, long chat," her dad explained. Abigail grew a little embarrassed and curious, suddenly forgetting about how bad she was feeling. She knew they had to talk one on one at some point. She wished she could snap her fingers and the worst part of it be over.

*It feels like going to the dentist,* she thought to herself.

Dad told them about a few things that happened and some of the things they talked about but didn't go into great detail. He was more interested in telling them about the fish that he'd caught. That made Abigail feel even more dread. Dad had spoken to Levi about something to do with her, and he wasn't telling her what it was. She leaned back in her chair in an attempt to relieve her aching back.

*This is going to bother me all day if I don't do something to forget about it.*

She instead decided to focus on the conversation that her mom started about what the pastor's wife was planning for the fall church picnic coming up in a few weeks.

She loved mornings like this with her parents. The three of them sitting comfortably and chatting about what was going on in life. She couldn't keep a smile from spreading across her face. Abigail was wise enough to treasure these times, especially after seeing how Dorothy's death had affected Levi. She could tell that he really regretted not spending more time with her.

Albert looked at his watch, reminding Abigail that she needed to do some paperwork regarding the Corbin case. She had to document how the Corbin boys were doing following Dorothy's will.

"I'm gonna have to take off," Abigail said, standing to her feet. She gulped the last bit of coffee that was in her cup and placed it in the sink. While she gathered her keys and purse, her mom told her dad about hearing sirens speed by their house that morning. But Abigail didn't remember hearing any sirens. Abigail furrowed her brow realizing she must have slept right through the racket. She shrugged it off and walked toward the door.

"Bye, Abby!" her mom called. Abigail returned a similar goodbye and let the door slam shut behind her. The air held a misty chill, and Abigail considered going back inside for a jacket but remembered that she'd left one in her car the previous day. The sun was high in the sky but was hidden by dark gray clouds. Despite the gloomy atmosphere, Abigail knew it wasn't supposed to rain and deemed it just another typical fall morning.

Abigail climbed into her car, started it, and began the slow trek down the driveway. When she stopped to look both ways before pulling out onto the road, her phone tweeted, letting her know that she'd received a text message. A quick glance told her it was from Levi. Strange, she didn't remember him sending her a text before this. He'd always called her. The message read:

*"This time he's gone too far."*

Abigail pushed her foot down on the gas pedal, sending her car speeding forward. She had to get to him. After everything that had happened, there was no telling what he meant by that.

Just before the Corbin house came into view, Abigail could see the flashing of lights bouncing off the trees. She sped up more until she could see police cars and an ambulance parked in the driveway of the Corbin house. Clouds of smoke slowly rose from the upper portion of the house. It looked like a small fire had started, probably causing damage to a few of the upstairs rooms. Abigail pulled her car in as close as she could to the house and ripped her keys from the ignition.

She ran to a group of people that were huddled in between some of the vehicles. Levi's face appeared among them, and Abigail slowed her speed from a run to a brisk walk. His eyes met hers and he turned to explain, but she didn't let him.

Instead, she threw her arms around his neck and kissed him. When she pulled her lips from his, he stared back into her eyes with a blank expression. She took a step back, trying to gain control of her emotions.

"I had no idea what I would find when I got here," she blurted out. It wasn't much of an explanation, but she thought it best to stick with it. He stuttered a bit, then started to ask her something, but she held up her hand and stopped him before he could begin.

"Just tell me what's going on here," she demanded. Levi looked at the ground, apparently trying to pull his mind back to the present situation.

"Well, I woke up this morning to a loud crash and a bang. I thought someone was in the house, so I preemptively called 911. I went to check out what it was and found that part of the attic and the two bedrooms on the far side of the house were on fire. The fire department came quickly, so there was minimal damage. Still, those rooms contained irreplaceable valuables. This was Silas' doing. It has to be."

Abigail listened intently to Levi, and when he'd finished explaining, she was able to control herself enough to give a response.

"I think you're right. It could have been Silas, but we will have to have proof before we start throwing out accusations," Abigail told him.

Levi smiled, obviously glad that she believed his suspicions.

"Do you remember yesterday when I took you to town and we saw Silas' driver, but Silas wasn't in the car?" Levi asked. She nodded in response.

"I think he had something to do with it," Levi continued. Abigail let her mind drift in thought for a moment.

"What would Silas have to gain by this?" she said out loud to herself. While she was still in thought, a police officer approached Levi.

"The fire department thinks they may have discovered what caused the fire," the officer said, motioning as a firefighter came forward holding a burned piece of metal pipe and cord with a small box attached to it.

"This looks like a contraption that was used to start a spark at a preset time near the highly flammable insulation. There is usually just the metal pipe left, but we got here faster than anticipated," the firefighter explained.

Levi shot a glance at Abigail.

"This was proof enough. It has to be," Levi whispered to her.

"I don't recommend you stay here until the damage can be repaired. We can place tarps over the doorways, and things from those rooms that can be salvaged to help keep the smoke out," the officer told him.

Levi stood motionless for a moment. Abigail was worried about what Levi might do; this was so much on him, and it pointed directly at Silas.

| 128 |

"You can stay with me if you want to," she heard herself say before she could stop herself.

*Lord, please let my parents be ok with this. What am I getting myself into?* Abigail was starting to question her sanity at this point.

"That's ok, I'll just go to the motel," Levi replied as the officer walked away.

"The only motel in town? Where Silas is staying?" Abigail added.

Levi admitted he hadn't thought of that. She knew he was trying to totally avoid Silas at this point.

"Yeah, you're probably right. I don't really want to see him right now," he said.

Abigail was relieved to hear him say that but had to tell him more legal jargon. "We will have to let him know of the damage since he is part owner," she explained.

Levi nodded and silently went to prepare his things for moving out.

"I will need help moving what's left of Grandma's things into storage, so they won't be destroyed by any potential damage in the future," he said over his shoulder.

Abigail agreed to help, following him into the house to give him a hand gathering his belongings.

The harsh smell of ash and soot assaulted her nose as soon as she walked in. Although the fire was put out before it could reach the staircase, the walls were blackened by the smoke that had been pulled out the front door when the firemen went inside. Abigail couldn't help the tears that rolled down her face. The generations that lived in this house, the wars it had been through, just to be destroyed by selfishness. She waited outside Levi's bedroom door and watched him repack the belongings that he'd brought with him.

Once Levi filled his suitcase, he took a long look around the room, and Abigail could see the memories playing back in his head. Then, without a word, he pushed his way past her and bounced down the stairs. She followed him, staying right on his heels and nearly running into him when he stopped by the front door.

"Can you give me a second?" he asked without looking at her. Abigail didn't reply but simply went to wait in her car. She watched as Levi locked up the house and started to head for his car.

Abigail continued watching Levi as he sat behind the wheel of his car and stared out into space. He then dropped his head on the backs of his hands. She caught sight of his body slightly rocking and dropped her head, feeling like she was invading his privacy by watching him weep for his childhood home. Abigail decided to direct her attention to the police officers and firefighters that were finishing their work.

One by one, the first responders disappeared from the property, and Abigail thought that since she'd already asked him out loud to stay with her, there wasn't any harm in trying again. She looked back over to see that Levi had finished crying and looked as if he felt a little better. Abigail stepped back out of her car and went over to his. Peering into his window, she smiled sympathetically.

"I really think you should come stay with me. My parents will insist anyway when they hear about this," she declared.

Reluctantly, Levi agreed.

She hurried back over to her car and climbed back into it, leading the little caravan down the road to the Wilson place.

*****

Levi felt a sense of dread and humiliation wash over him, like everything that made him feel some sort of connection with his grandma was being slowly taken away from him. Maybe that was what Silas had had in mind from the beginning. Levi didn't know exactly how his cousin was responsible for the damage at the house but felt determined to find out. In the meantime, he was going to have to find a way to get out of the embarrassment that Silas had caused him yet again.

Before Levi knew it, he had his car parked in front of the Wilson house. It reminded him of a few days before, when the officer came out to tell him that Silas had nearly murdered someone. At that time, he had a place to stay and he was at this house as a respectable guest. He was able to make a good impression and had some dignity. Now? Levi felt like he was a nobody asking for a handout.

He stepped out of the car, not sure if he should take his suitcase out until Abigail spoke with her family about it.

Levi watched her slowly slide out of her car. She approached him with a look of nervousness in her eyes.

"Give me just a minute to explain to my parents what's going on," Abigail commanded with a pleading tone.

"Sure," was all Levi could say. She turned and hurried into the house. He noticed that she wasn't walking the way she normally did; she didn't have that brisk stride with her head held high, demanding respect through the dignity and beauty that was held in her face. Abigail was in the house for several minutes before she came back out again, this time with Albert and Nancy following her. Nancy approached him with a look of compassion and concern on her face. The look of a mother Levi had yearned for since he was a boy.

"Levi, are you alright, dear? Thank heaven you weren't hurt," she said, clasping her hands together as if she was thanking God right where she stood.

"Let me get your bags," Albert offered, heading straight for the back of his car.

"Bag. I have one bag," Levi corrected, pressing the button on his key ring, causing the trunk to open like magic. Albert grabbed Levi's suitcase and grunted as he carried it inside. Levi quickly turned around to tell him that he didn't have to do that, but Albert spoke first.

"Just remember that you are now a guest in our home

and will be treated as one." It was as if Albert had read his thoughts. Levi silently followed the family into the house before grabbing Abigail by the shoulder, turning her face towards his. Now that he had a closer look at her, Levi could see that she was a little pale and her breathing was heavier than normal.

"Are you feeling ok?" he asked. She looked up at him and he noticed that her eyes were starting to water.

"Actually, no," she mumbled, rubbing her nose.

"I think you may have a cold. There's been a lot going on lately. Maybe you need a day off," Levi said with a look of concern on his face.

Abigail simply nodded in agreement. "I'm gonna go back to bed, then. I'll see you later," she said as she trudged up the stairs and disappeared.

"I put your suitcase in the guest bedroom, Levi," Albert announced.

"Thank you very much," Levi replied, sitting in the living room so he could mentally plan how he was going to handle the situation. He tapped his kneecaps with the palms of his hands in nervous thought. A few moments later, Nancy appeared from the kitchen with a steaming mug in her hand before heading upstairs. Levi suspected that she was checking on Abigail. A minute later, Albert came into the living room and sat across from him.

"I know the person that Dorothy insured the house through. I'll talk with him today," he assured Levi.

"Thank you, but I don't think this was an accident," Levi declared.

"I don't either. I know that house meant everything to Dorothy, and she spared no expense keeping it in great shape. We'll get to the bottom of this," Albert promised.

Levi paused a moment, then began to explain to him about the contraption that was found in the attic. "One of the firefighters said that there is only supposed to be the lead pipe left, but it didn't burn like it was supposed to, and they got there quickly."

Albert's eyes widened at the information, but Levi couldn't tell if it was from surprise or delight. He watched in surprise as Albert jumped to his feet and grabbed his car keys.

"Tell Nancy that I'll be back later," he commanded as he hurried out the door.

*****

Silas couldn't wait to make his big entrance at the house. He would find it all burned to the ground, contact the insurance company, collect half of the money, and be out of town before the end of the week. Silas just hoped that everything would work out without them being caught. After all, there should be no sign left of the contraption Clayton had built. As they were preparing to leave the motel room, Silas caught sight of a familiar face getting out of a parked car just below their room.

Dread filled him as he realized it was Albert Wilson. Something must have gone wrong for him to be here.

Silas was ready to think the worst had happened, but he stopped himself; there was no point in thinking that way until he was sure about what'd happened. When Albert made his way up the stairs to the second floor of the motel, Silas was still standing in the doorway. Albert approached him, keeping a few feet of space between them. Silas looked behind Albert to see Clayton standing just out of sight, fully aware of what was going on. Silas was glad that he didn't make his presence known to Albert.

"Silas, you didn't let me state my business when you were in jail, so I've come to state it now. I want to represent you in court." Albert's tone had nothing suspicious about it, but Silas wasn't going to chance it. He wasn't simply going to trust that Albert had come here without wearing a wire. He looked back at Clayton who gave him a nod.

"Why don't you come inside, and we'll talk about it," Silas offered as he stepped outside of the doorway. He held his hands out, gesturing him inside like he was an honored guest. Albert shook his head.

"No, thank you. I know you're willing to do whatever it takes to get what you want, and I've dealt with many men like that one," he nodded toward the direction of a hidden Clayton.

"I'd feel more comfortable stating my business out here with witnesses," Albert replied, waving his hand behind him. Silas looked over his shoulder to see one of the motel maids coming around the corner with her cleaning cart.

"The truth is out, Silas," Albert stated. "Everyone knows what you and your friend did to your grandma's house. With that and the charges that will be brought against you regarding Bella Rodriguez, your court-appointed attorney won't help you whatsoever."

Silas wanted to get angry at the information Albert brought to him, but he had to wonder. If Albert knew he was so guilty, and that no lawyer would touch him, then why did he want to help him? So, Silas asked just that.

"Because of your grandmother. She had high hopes for you and prayed for you all the time," Albert replied.

Silas laughed. "No, she didn't. She was glad whenever I went home to my parents."

"What made you think that?"

"Because I would hear her tell Levi that they were going to do things when I left. Fun things. She never loved me. Levi was always her favorite."

"Did she ever not include you while you stayed with her?" Albert asked him.

Silas closed the door behind him, so Albert couldn't see into his room. He leaned on the rail, not wanting to look Albert in the face. After some thought, he shook his head in response, finding it hard to admit the truth.

"She always tried to include me, but it always felt forced." Silas' voice cracked a little.

"Did it ever occur to you that it was hard for her to see you go?" Albert asked as he leaned on the rail as well.

Silas wanted to think there was some love for him in his grandma's heart, but there couldn't possibly be after he left the last time and never looked back.

Albert began to tell him about how they could change his life if he faced his problems like a man. Silas needed to face the fact that he'd assaulted Bella. He couldn't run from his problems forever and now was as good a time as any to face them. He'd done wrong and needed to pay for it.

"I know you will have prison time, but I also know about forgiveness. All I can do is simply urge you to turn yourself in," Albert finished.

Silas wanted to believe him. He wanted a new life, but Albert had no idea what he was running from. The police would catch up with him sooner or later, and he was out of money. Silas had nowhere to go.

He doubted that Clayton would stay with him; he was loyal to his boss. Either way, Silas knew his running was over. Should he just go to prison and accept what was coming, or should he try to make amends before going to prison?

*I have a lot to think about.*

Levi drove along the twisted back road, thinking about the events of the morning. It felt like they had taken place days ago instead of just a few hours. His head felt foggy, and a dull pain throbbed in his forehead. Levi rubbed it gently in hopes of some relief, but it didn't help. Despite his head hurting, though, he was glad that he couldn't smell smoke on himself anymore.

Nancy had been kind enough to let him take a shower in the downstairs bathroom, so he didn't wake Abigail. Truth be told, Levi felt strange not having seen Abigail all day. He had spent almost every day with her since his arrival and hated to think of her not feeling well.

After getting cleaned up, Levi thought it was a good idea to get out of the house—to get his mind off Abigail. He decided he would go to the hospital and see how Bella was doing.

The colorful trees flew past him in a blur of oranges, yellows, and browns. Levi rolled down his window to smell the crisp fall air. When he had hopped on the train, he had expected to come here for some time alone to mourn Grandma, but that was the last thing he was getting.

As Levi drifted past Grandma's house, he didn't look at it. It was too difficult to see the blackened window and missing wall scarring up the entire east side of the house. He also tried to keep Silas out of his mind but couldn't. *How could he do this?* Levi asked himself that question over and over but couldn't think of a good answer. He hated Silas even more for what he had done to Grandma's precious house.

Levi remembered the vision he'd had about the Native Americans rowing down the river behind Grandma's house. How Silas had killed all of them. He hadn't considered it before he came to town, but now he believed that Silas wasn't above killing. Levi then thought about the conversation that he'd had with Albert.

*"The root of bitterness,"* Albert's voice echoed through his mind. Albert had acted as if bitterness was a horrible poison, but was it really that big of a deal? Levi knew that bitterness could take happiness out of life, but he wasn't to that point yet. He couldn't be, not with how he felt when he was around Abigail. Plus, if he tried to change things between himself and Silas, it would likely blow up in his face.

Levi paused for a moment, surprised with the argument he made in his mind. He'd just considered mending his relationship with Silas, if even for only a moment. Maybe there wasn't as much bitterness inside him as Albert thought. He turned his car into the large parking lot of the hospital and quickly found a parking spot, allowing himself a few seconds of glee that he was able to snag a spot close to the door.

As he walked into the hospital, Levi made a mental map of the route so he could make it back to Bella's room without having to ask a nurse for directions.

*Wow, maybe that stereotype about men was true after all.* He smirked to himself.

Levi went to the elevator where he'd followed Abigail just a few days ago. Once inside, he pressed the large button with a three on it, making it light up, and let the doors slowly close.

While he waited for the elevator to make the climb, he thought about all the times he'd tried to find his way and avoided asking for help. Levi remembered being at the library when he was fourteen, trying to find some books about cars.

Levi had circled the library more than five times before he discovered that he'd walked past them several times without realizing it. So many memories were brought back to him since he came to town.

*Maybe things weren't so bad here,* he reasoned.

When the elevator doors opened, he took a left and remembered the door that he'd walked through before.

Next to the door was a large sign on the wall that read 315.

"315D," he said under his breath. Levi walked out of the elevator and past 315A and 315B. Down the hall was a man standing just outside a room. He had jet black hair and a wrinkled windbreaker jacket. His face was buried in his hands. Levi could hear the sobs from where he was standing and approached the man, compassionately placing a hand on his shoulder.

"Excuse me, sir. Are you Mr. Rodriguez?" Levi asked. The man lifted his face and looked at Levi. His dark brown eyes looked exactly like Bella's, and Levi knew there was no question that he was her father.

"Yes," the man replied, trying to pull his emotions back together.

"My name is Levi Corbin. I'm a friend of Bella's," Levi said.

The man's face darkened when he heard Levi's last name. "Corbin!? Are you the animal that did this to my little girl?!" he growled. The man charged at him like a bull, tightly wrapping his fingers around Levi's throat. Levi gasped for air and shoved the man back. The man stumbled, and before he could regain his footing, Levi held up his hands in surrender. The gesture seemed to do the trick in calming him down, and the man stopped in his tracks.

"No, I didn't hurt her," Levi wheezed. "My good-for-nothing cousin did. We just have the same last name." Levi saw a flash of alarm on the man's face as the realization of what was going on hit him. Knowing that the man was about to apologize, Levi decided to save him the trouble under the circumstances.

"It's alright," he said with a cough. The man's face was flushed from when he had been crying, but Levi figured the rage he'd just displayed on his face was also a contributing factor.

"I'm so sorry. I don't know what came over me," he said, wiping the already drying tears from his face.

"I do. Your daughter is in critical condition. I don't even consider Silas family after this," Levi replied, straightening his shirt collar.

The man stuck out his hand for Levi's. "Quinn Rodriguez," he stated.

Levi grabbed the proffered hand and received a firm handshake.

Quinn released his hand and pointed to the door of the room, which contained a window. A woman sat in the room with Bella. She had jet black hair that trailed down her back, and her face was distorted from the sobs that Levi could hear even with the door closed.

"That is my wife Mila," he explained.

Levi's heart tore for the woman; he couldn't imagine what she was feeling.

"Bella was put on life support this morning due to a stroke that was caused by bleeding in her brain.

The doctors don't think she will make it," Quinn said softly.

Levi felt numb for a moment, and it took him several

minutes to process what he'd just heard. He felt like he was in some way responsible for this.

*How could he do something like this?! Bella is going to die because of Silas. How could I have considered forgiving him?*

Despair tore through his chest.

"I'm so sorry," was all he managed to get out. Levi turned his gaze to Quinn's wife, wishing there was something he could do.

A few minutes later, Levi left the hospital, feeling a great sense of defeat. He had no idea what to expect from here on out. Bella was dying because of Silas. Grandma's house was nearly destroyed because of Silas. And Abigail was sick at home, but he couldn't really blame that on Silas, even though he wanted to.

All Levi knew was that he didn't want to go back to the Wilson house just yet. He needed to take some time to think things over and figure out what to do next. As he pulled out of the hospital parking lot, he saw a small advertisement for Taylormade Coffee. Coffee sounded excellent. After the challenge of navigating his way through town, Levi ended up getting a parking spot right in front of the front door of the coffee shop.

He looked across the street, catching a glimpse of the Wilson law firm. Levi started to think about his first meeting with Abigail. *No*, he reminded himself. He needed to think about other things. Levi pulled out the small black book he kept in his shirt pocket and flipped through the pages. The last thing he had written in it was from the day he met Abigail:

*I hope that we can get this over with soon.*

That hope was long gone. Levi entered the coffee shop, greeted by the delicious smells of maple, sugar, and coffee. He couldn't help but love the atmosphere. It was trendy, relaxing, and had a wholesome feel. There were two older men sitting in a booth laughing and talking, and a few teens scattered here and there with laptops and magazines. Although each person was in their own little world, they all had one thing in common. Coffee. Levi approached the counter and mentally prepared to place his order. As he felt in his pocket for a pen, he looked up to see an old woman arguing with a teenage boy that was standing behind the counter.

"I want a maple latte with *two* sugars and *extra* cream. Now, I'm going over to sit at that table. Can you bring me my order in a timely manner?" she barked at him, pointing to the empty table beside Levi. The boy timidly nodded and hurried to meet her demands. As she turned, Levi noticed a small gold medal hanging around her neck; it reminded him of Grant's medal. To help get his mind on the medal and deciphering the clues to finding it, Levi made a quick sketch of what he imagined the medal to look like. After that he wrote down the clues that he and Abigail had gathered to get a visual perspective.

He heard the old woman grunt and groan as she made her way over to the seat she'd announced was hers. She plopped herself down, and in a few seconds, the young boy brought her a steaming coffee mug. She picked it up and took a few sips from it.

The woman must have snuck a peek at what Levi was writing because she patted him on the shoulder.

"You are interested in our great General Grant? I know a good deal about him. I am a member of the local historical society, and we pride ourselves on knowing about our heritage," she said.

Levi looked at the woman, wanting to tell her that he was busy but slapped his little book closed to prevent her from reading more. Judging by what he'd heard from her at the counter, he didn't want to get on her bad side.

"I'm Violet Beetle," she said, sticking a puffy, pale hand out to him. He grabbed it, unsure if he should shake it for fear that he would hurt her. Touching her made her seem frailer than the feisty woman that was barking orders to the barista just a few moments ago.

"Levi. Levi Corbin," he told her.

Violet lit up when she heard his name. "You're one of Dorothy's grandsons? You're not the one who killed that girl, are you?" she gasped.

"No, ma'am," Levi replied, inwardly sighing. It was easy to forget just how fast news traveled in a small town.

"Good. What an awful thing to happen. And to one of our own girls, too," her hand raised to touch a cheek in dismay.

Levi decided it was best not to correct her. She had so

many details that were not true that it would take him all day to set her straight.

Violet took another sip from her mug. "I knew Dorothy from the historical society. She was a very smart lady," she said.

"Yes, she was," Levi agreed.

"The whole group tried to convince her to join the Daughters of the Revolution group because of how much she knew about her own history. Since you are interested in General Grant, you should come down and have a look at our records collections," Violet offered. Levi faked a smile.

"I'll have to do that sometime," he told her. Levi realized that he would probably have to leave to get anything accomplished today.

*So much for coming here to think,* he thought, forcing himself to be polite.

"Oh, how wonderful! You're continuing your grandmother's legacy," Violet pulled a white handkerchief from her purse and blew her dainty nose.

Levi faked another smile and gathered his things. *Did the thought of that really make her cry?* She seemed like she was acting, and Levi wasn't sure he trusted her.

"Well, I'd better be going," he announced.

She reached in her purse again and pulled out a card. "If you ever want to talk about Dorothy or have any questions about the society, give me a call," she said, holding it out. Levi got an uneasy feeling at that announcement. She couldn't possibly know about the medal, could she? Should he ask her? Or should he wait and ask Abigail about her? Levi decided on the latter and took the card. As he left he was tempted to turn and look back at the woman but waited until he was outside before glancing in the window at her. She was on a cell phone. Levi hurried to his car and started back to the Wilsons' house.

*****

Abigail felt like she was stuck in a gray marsh. She couldn't move her body and could barely breathe.

*Where am I?* A warm sensation tingled on her right arm, and Abigail focused all her attention on that spot in the hope that, somehow, she'd be able to move. Then she heard something.

"Abby," someone said her name in a whisper. It seemed close, but it was too hard to hear clearly.

"Abby, can you hear me?" they called out again. Abigail definitely heard it that time and was desperate to answer, to ask for help, but she didn't know what she could do to let them know she heard them. Her body suddenly began to shake as fear rose in her chest. Then, a bright light shone over her head. Shapes started to appear. A face.

"Abby, dear, wake up!" Nancy shook her shoulders gently. Relief washed over Abigail when she realized it was all a dream that her mother had, thankfully, rescued her from.

"Huh?" was all she managed to get out as her mind began to clear the cobwebs. Her mother shook her again as if dusting the last bit of sleep off of her.

"Abby, Levi wants to talk to you," Nancy said gently. Abigail opened her eyes wide to clear her vision.

"Um, ok," she muttered. Nancy stepped away from the bed and began tidying up the room absentmindedly. Abigail looked at the door, and her cheeks flushed when she saw that Levi was already standing there. He had seen her sleeping and her unattractive attempts to wake herself up. Abigail felt vulnerable sitting in bed, not knowing how her face and hair looked. Her mom could have given her a few minutes of warning before bringing him in, at least.

"Hi," she chirped, trying to at least sound attractive.

Levi smiled, giving a pointed look in Nancy's direction to convey that he wanted to speak with Abigail privately. She looked at Levi and then her mother and immediately caught the hint.

"Mom, I'm really getting hungry. Can you go make us some lunch?" Abigail asked.

Nancy turned to look at her daughter, her expression clearly saying, *I want to stay and listen.*

"Alright, I'll go make us all some lunch." Nancy gave in, sighing as she glided out of the room. "But that door stays open," she called over her shoulder.

Abigail let her head drop into her palm.

"I'm sorry about that," she grumbled. Levi placed a caring hand on her shoulder, causing Abigail to look back up at him. Her stomach fluttered as she stared into his kind eyes.

"First, how are you feeling?" he asked her. She couldn't help but smile.

"I'm feeling better, but you should step back in case I'm contagious," she warned.

"I'll take my chances," Levi smiled back, keeping his hand on her shoulder.

"What was it you needed to talk to me about?" Abigail asked, attempting to break the moment they were sharing. She was having a difficult time fighting the urge to kiss him. Levi seemed to read her thoughts because he quickly removed his hand and took a step back.

"I just came to ask you if you know a lady named Violet Beetle," Levi said.

Abigail's head shot up. "You met the Beetle?" she asked, holding up her hands as if she was trying to be scary. Levi seemed surprised at her response, and the nickname, so Abigail began to explain. "She's a bit of an old kook in that she always tried to act just like your grandmother. The Beetle hung around Dorothy all the time and even joined the historical group, following after your grandmother. You could see that your grandmother put up with her to be nice but didn't care for her company."

Levi told her of his experience with Violet at the coffee shop and how she'd terrorized some young teenager that worked there. "I had no memory of her at all until you just called her the Beetle. That's the only name the kids used for her. I guess I never knew her real name until today," Levi chuckled at the realization.

"I can't believe I didn't put the two together."

"She is notorious for terrorizing kids," Abigail commented. She folded her hands and placed them in her lap.

"It was strange. I felt like she knew something about the history of my house, to the point that I'm pretty sure she even said something about the medal," Levi said.

Abigail felt her face scrunch up with concern. "How would she even know about that?" she asked.

"I was wondering the same thing. Maybe my grandma told her about it."

"No, I knew your grandma very well, and I know she didn't particularly care for Violet. Dorothy wouldn't tell the Beetle about something so important to her," Abigail told him.

Levi raised his eyebrows as if saying that he hadn't considered that.

Abigail waited for him to say something else, but he didn't. Soon the silence between them began to make things uncomfortable, and she was afraid that that was all he wanted to ask her about. Then she got the warm sensation that he was looking at her.

"How are you feeling?" he asked, causing her cheeks to flush again.

"Better, but Mom thinks I shouldn't go back to work until tomorrow," Abigail said. She could see in his eyes that there was something he wasn't telling her. Something horrible. "Levi, is something wrong?" she asked, grabbing his hand.

He returned the grip. "I went to see Bella. Her parents made it to town and are with her." Levi then closed his mouth as if to keep the words from escaping.

Abigail felt a flood of emotions applying pressure to her chest and throat. She had an idea of what he might say but wasn't sure that she wanted to hear the words he was holding back.

"Bella had a stroke from bleeding in the brain, and they don't think she will make it," Levi continued after a moment.

Abigail had to run those words through her mind a few times so that her brain could properly process them. Bella was going to die. Tears began to roll down her cheeks as she thought about the girl's parents coming to town to say goodbye to their child. Although she didn't know the young girl very well, Abigail felt like she was losing a friend or a little sister.

"Thank you for telling me," she whispered.

"I thought you'd want to know," he said, standing to his feet.

Abigail threw the covers off herself and began climbing out of bed.

"What are you doing?" Levi asked.

"I need to go see her," she announced as she grabbed some clothes from her closet and started toward the bathroom across from her bed.

Levi grabbed her arm and pulled her back to him.

"I really think they need to be alone with her. These are the last few hours they will have with her," he explained.

Abigail wanted to pull away and go regardless. She wanted to see if there was anything she could do to help them, but she knew he was right. Dejectedly, Abigail buried her face in his chest, and he wrapped his arms around her. Tears began to fall from her eyes again, and Levi squeezed her as if he could read her mind. It was at that moment that Abigail realized that she'd fallen in love with Levi despite her best efforts not to.

"Um, I hope I'm interrupting something," said a voice from the doorway. Abigail and Levi both froze and glanced at the door, only to see Albert standing there.

CHAPTER

12

As Silas lay in the poor excuse for a bed that the motel offered, he considered everything that Albert Wilson had said to him. Should he turn himself in? He felt like that was a terrible idea and wouldn't do him any good, but Silas had always heard it made things easier in court. He was tired of running and knew that if he continued with this lifestyle it likely would result in his death. But at this point, he knew he deserved whatever came. Silas climbed out of the bed and made his way over to the large, musty curtains that shielded the room from the world. He pulled them back and stared out the window.

The curtains smelled like smoke even though this room was non-smoking, betraying the cheap cleaning efforts and age of the room itself. This motel wasn't as nice as the other motels they had stayed at before they came to Granton, but what little money Silas had was finally gone, and now they were staying here on Clayton's dime.

As he looked outside, Silas took in the view with a heavy sigh. There was a street that paralleled the motel and another street that created an intersection, making it so that Silas could see down for several streets. A few blocks away, some young boys were playing basketball in the street. Silas envied them; they had no worries. If he could only go back in time, he would better appreciate those years.

The room was quiet without Clayton, who had left an hour or so ago to meet with someone in town. He wouldn't say what for, but it was probably to convey the situation here, and he was now on his way to New York.

Since Albert's visit to their motel, Clayton had demanded that they forget about the house and leave town before they were both arrested. But Silas had managed to convince him that they would leave early the next morning, that they still had time before the police found them here. It gave Silas time to think things over, and if he decided to turn himself in, he would go alone.

Despite sounding as if he had undeniable proof, Silas somehow knew that Albert wouldn't turn him in, at least not at this point. Silas wasn't exactly trying to hide anyway. This was the only motel in town and their car was easily recognizable. He didn't think they would make it very far if they tried to run. He didn't even feel like trying.

"You may want to take a step back from the window,"

Clayton barked at him as he burst into the room. Silas jumped, startled that he came out of nowhere so quietly. He turned toward the door with a twinge of anger growing inside him.

"What's your problem?" Silas barked back.

"I don't know why you're wanting to stick around here. That guy seemed to have no trouble finding us, and he said that the cops know it was us that burned the house down. There's nothing left here," Clayton explained.

Deep down, Silas didn't want to believe that. He no longer wanted this life but had no idea how to get out of it. Albert Wilson was the first and only person willing to show him how.

"I still have things to take care of. If you're so worried, then go," Silas pointed toward the door. Just a few days ago he had considered this man the only friend he had in the world, despite the reason he was with him. But now? Silas just wanted to get away from him as soon as possible. He wasn't sure when or how the change had happened, but suddenly he realized it had.

"I'm not coming back for you," Clayton stated after a pause. The words hurt a little, but Clayton must've had some idea of what Silas was considering. Clayton grabbed the bag that he had prepared in case of trouble showing up, looked Silas in the eye, then turned without a word and walked out the door.

Silas wanted to stop him and ask him to stay, but he knew that things were different now, and he knew what he had to do. Still standing at the window, Silas watched as Clayton walked down the long, open corridor and down to the first floor where the parking lot was just outside of the door. He watched as Clayton climbed into the shiny black car and sped off.

Silas let his head drop. All the emotions he'd carried for years felt like they were getting heavier, and he didn't want to carry them anymore. To have a life like Levi's was all he'd ever wanted, but that was something Silas would never have. Now was the time. He turned and went back to the bed where he had been lying and sat on the edge facing the window once again. Silas looked at the old rotary phone that sat on the nightstand. He'd never thought in a million years that he would be doing this.

He picked up the receiver and placed it to his ear. The dial tone played in his mind a scene of police cars racing down the street, forcing the young boys that were playing basketball to the sidewalk and disrupting the peaceful neighborhood. Silas paused. He felt like he'd caused enough trouble in this town and decided that he would walk to the police station himself.

For the last time before being locked away, Silas would enjoy the outdoors. He grabbed the bag that was on the floor next to the bathroom door and went down to the office where an older woman sat behind a tall counter. Her line of sight was so low that she could barely see over, but she looked up at him anyway.

"Can I help you?"

"Just checking out," Silas muttered, tossing the keys to his room onto the counter. She typed and clicked a few times on a computer that was hidden behind the counter almost as well as she was.

"You're ready to go," the lady said, handing him a receipt.

*Not really*, Silas thought to himself as he looked the receipt over. He wondered if he should find a way to get this to Clayton or not, but in the end, he had no idea where Clayton was going. A small part of him wished he had gone with him after all.

"Are you alright?" the woman asked.

Silas looked up at her confused. "Excuse me?" he asked.

"You look like you've just lost everything," the woman replied.

"Well, I guess you could say that I have," he said back.

Slowly, the receptionist came around the counter, revealing that she had part of her leg missing. She had a unique wooden cane that she placed aside to give him a hug that was both fragile and also the biggest he had ever received. Silas awkwardly patted the woman on the shoulder, thinking that she might be crazy.

"This is where you can start again," she said with a loving smile. Those words went right through Silas, touching him to his core. He was viewing the situation as if his life was over, and this woman was telling him that this could be the start. She had no idea what she was talking about, but considering the wrinkled face that smiled back at him and the part of her leg that was missing, maybe she knew more than he thought.

*****

Levi didn't know what to say when he saw Albert standing in the doorway, but he nearly panicked anyway. It was plain to see that the door was wide open, so nothing inappropriate was happening, and Abigail's tearstained face should have been a clear indicator as to why he was holding her. Still, he knew they were in an awkward spot.

"Dad, Mom was in here a minute ago, and he was telling me about Bella's condition," Abigail tried to explain. Albert just waved his hand, motioning for Levi to follow him down the hallway. Abigail tried to follow but was stopped by Albert's voice.

"Stay there. I need to talk to him alone for a moment," Albert commanded.

Levi felt like a fish was flopping inside of his stomach. He really enjoyed being here and didn't want to be kicked out due to a misunderstanding. Albert led him into the guest room where he'd been told he could stay that morning. After Albert closed the bedroom door behind him, he stood toe to toe with Levi.

After a few moments of silence, Levi decided that he would try again to defend himself and Abigail and convey that they had done nothing wrong. "Look, Mr. Wilson, Grandma raised me to be a gentleman. I know how to act, and I have the highest respect for your house and your daughter," he muttered. Levi felt that Albert might as well have a gun on him. After all, it was an old, local custom to shoot a young man that was found in an unmarried woman's bedroom.

"I was telling Abigail that the word is Bella isn't going to make it. The family has been advised to consider making funeral arrangements," Levi continued to explain.

Albert held up his hand to stop him.

"I have some news for you," Albert announced.

Levi paused, not expecting this sort of response or the strange expression Albert wore.

"Silas has decided to turn himself in. He will be giving a full confession regarding the house, and he will also be giving a statement regarding that poor girl in the hospital," he continued.

"How do you know this?" Levi asked, as nerves tickled his stomach. He doubted that Silas was sorry for what he'd done and wondered if this was another one of his attempts to look like the victim.

Albert slid his hands into his pockets. "He called me and told me himself while he was on his way to the police station."

"So, since you decided to defend him, you two are all buddy-buddy now?" Levi could feel his anger rising, and he no longer cared if Albert could see the bitterness and anger on his face. "I don't know what this is supposed to mean to me, or even why you're telling me, but let me tell you that Silas cannot be trusted."

"Maybe he doesn't know how to win someone else's trust. It's plain to see that you've never tried to help him learn," Albert reasoned. Levi was taken aback by the comment. He felt like he was being betrayed.

"I shouldn't have to. I was the one who was orphaned. I had enough problems of my own," Levi's emotions were getting the better of him. Tears threatened to come, and he blinked faster to fight them. He was hearing the words come out of his mouth but was powerless to stop them.

"Sounds to me like you still have them," Albert retorted as he turned to walk out of the room. When the door shut, Levi plopped down on the bed. He thought about the other day when he and Albert were sitting by the river. *The Root of Bitterness.* Those words were starting to make more and more sense to him.

*****

Abigail stood in the center of her bedroom where Levi had been holding her. She had no idea how she was going to explain this to her dad, and she had always wanted nothing but the highest respect from him. Her bedroom door was still open, and Abigail could hear the muffled voices of Levi and Albert through the bedroom wall. The guest room had once been her brother George's room, and the wall that their rooms shared used to be the source of many fights and many games. Abigail remembered when they had learned about Morse code in school. She and George learned it perfectly and would use it to communicate through the wall.

After a few moments, Abigail heard George's door open and close, followed by footsteps leading down the hall. It sounded like only one person had left, but who was it? Did Levi stay in the room or did her dad? Albert often liked to go in there and sit among George's things; he said it made him feel closer to his son.

Abigail tiptoed to her door in time to see the back of her dad's balding head disappear into the kitchen. That meant Levi was still in George's room. She went and tapped on the door. Without a word, Levi opened it and she stepped inside.

"Look, we can explain everything to them at lunch and how nothing happened or was going to happen," Abigail blurted out. Levi had a look on his face that Abigail hated to see there. It was partly sadness and anger mixed with a little bit of disappointment.

*What did Dad tell him?*

"Are you ok?" she asked after a pause.

"Apparently your dad and Silas are best friends. He's convinced Silas to turn himself in, confess to arson, and give his statement on what happened with Bella," Levi's voice dripped with bitterness.

"No, Levi, there are certain steps that need to be taken with a person whose guilt is definite. My dad is not the type to make things up and lie, so he has other methods for handling cases like this," Abigail tried to explain softly.

Levi went to the bed and plopped down on it. She wasn't sure if he was going to cry or not, but she knew that this time she'd better stay by the door.

"I still don't understand why your dad wants to help him. He really deserves everything that's coming to him, but now he'll walk away without having learned anything," Levi grumbled angrily.

"He won't get off scot-free for this. I really think you need to see what my dad's trying to do with Silas. I didn't understand why he was doing this at first either, but it's mostly for your grandmother. She loved Silas just as much as she loved you, and it pained her to see his life going the way it is." Abigail walked over to Levi and gave him a quick hug. He looked up at her almost as if he was asking her to stay with him, but she couldn't. She needed to get away from him for a little while to think.

"I hope you find peace about this at some point. Technically, Silas still owns half of that house until he pleads guilty in court to arson. Then, it's all yours, and the medal too. Maybe that will make you happy."

She exited the room, leaving him sitting alone on the bed. Abigail hated to see Levi dealing with all the raw emotions from his childhood. Part of her wanted to comfort him and tell him that everything would work itself out, but the other part of her wanted to shake him and tell him that he needed to let this go so he could move on and be happy.

She had to question herself for having feelings for him so quickly. Abigail didn't want to be with a man that was so consumed by hatred and bitterness. She wanted him to always wear that smile she had seen him wear when he was first at her house.

Abigail stopped by her bedroom, picked up her fluffy, purple bathrobe, eased it on and tied the rope around her waist. She then slipped her feet into some warm, cozy socks and went downstairs to see if there was any way she could help her mother. Levi needed to be left alone for a while, and she really needed to distance herself from him.

CHAPTER

13

———————————

Levi rolled over on the lumpy mattress. His chest felt heavy due to the events of the day. He was emotionally exhausted and didn't feel like eating. It wouldn't have mattered anyway, being so late, and with the Wilson family already in bed asleep, but Levi didn't feel like sleeping either. His body ached from lying still for the last few hours, but he couldn't think of anything better to do. Maybe he could try to go over the clues again to see if he'd missed anything. He had really wanted to find that medal just a few hours ago, but now it didn't seem as important anymore.

Silas was already out of the picture for good, and the house would be his. That was what Levi wanted, wasn't it? Maybe finding the medal would prove something to himself and Abigail, but he doubted it. Still, he reached over to where his jacket hung over a chair that sat next to the bed and felt through it for his little black notebook. Levi hadn't had a chance to go over the clues much at Taylor made Coffee because of Violet Beetle, so now seemed as good a time as any. Instead of going through and trying to deduce from their findings, he pulled out his little pencil and began writing.

*Things just seem to be going from bad to worse, and I don't feel like writing about everything that has happened in the last few days. I want to sleep but can't. Somehow, Silas seems to be some sort of lost puppy in everyone else's eyes, and I've become a cruel, heartless jerk. I know what Silas has done in the past, and I know you're supposed to let the past go, but how? No one knows for sure if he's really in jail anyway. It could all be just another act.*

Levi considered this thought. Maybe Silas wasn't in jail at all and just told people he was. That wouldn't be outrageous, given his personality. He leaned up sharply, slapped his notebook closed, and gently pulled the jacket off the chair to avoid knocking the chair over. Levi then tiptoed to the doorway and slowly pulled the door open. It let out a long creaking sound that seemed to shake the whole house. A small part of him wanted to wake up Abigail and see if she would go with him, but he thought it best if he didn't. Levi remembered Albert's expression when he was standing in the doorway of her bedroom, and he didn't want to mar Abigail's reputation any more.

He continued through the house and down the stairs. Making his way outside, Levi took a deep breath of the cool night air. Yes, this was exactly what he needed. He climbed into his car, started the engine and drove the car out of the driveway.

As he started down the road to town, Abigail's words echoed in his mind.

*"I hope you find peace about this at some point."*

That was something Levi had never considered. Not only did he not have peace in this situation with Silas, but he also did not have peace within himself. Was it from being orphaned? Did it have something to do with Grandma? Maybe he should consider therapy when he returned home to Ohio. With those thoughts in mind, Levi searched his memory to try and remember where he'd seen the jailhouse when he got reacquainted with Granton a few days ago. The jailhouse was one place he didn't have much memory of due to grandma making sure he stayed out of trouble as a child. He'd never even seen it up close before.

It had to be somewhere near the grocery store. As the city lights came into view, Levi started paying close attention for any signs or landmarks that would give him a hint of where the jail could be. It wasn't long before he found it near the grocery store, just like he'd remembered. Levi pulled his car into the parking lot, quickly climbed out, and strode into the building. Once he stepped inside, a bright fluorescent light greeted him. Levi had to squint a bit until his eyes adjusted and he could make out a heavy-set woman in uniform behind a reception desk.

"Excuse me, do you have a Silas Corbin in here?" he asked quietly.

"Visiting hours are over," she replied without looking up from the papers that spread out in front of her.

"I'm not here for a visit, I'm just wondering if he is here," Levi replied.

The woman sighed, pulled a clipboard from the desk drawer, and gently lifted one of the pages. "Silas Corbin?" she asked.

"Yes, ma'am," he replied.

"Yeah, we have Mr. Corbin here."

"Thank you," Levi said with a sigh, turning to leave.

"Hold up. What's your name?" the officer asked sternly, her tone suggesting that he answer her question to avoid any trouble.

"Levi. Levi Corbin," he said, suddenly regretting that he'd come. The woman wrote down his name and asked for a contact phone number. He gave her his cell phone number and left as quickly as he could before she could ask him anything else.

Stepping outside, it was difficult to see with the single blinding streetlight in the parking lot. As he waited for his eyes to adjust to the night, he figured he'd better get back to Abigail's house before they noticed he was gone. Levi fished his car keys from his pocket, but just before he could put them in the door of the car, he heard foot-steps behind him.

He turned and did his best not to let out a loud gasp, but no one was there. That was when he noticed a few small trees that stood next to the parking lot. He wasn't sure, but it looked like someone was standing behind one of them about thirty yards away. Levi took a few steps closer and saw the figure start moving its way down the street. It was tiptoeing and crouching over, trying not to be seen. Levi followed.

He watched as the figure made its way down the block and stopped in front of a house. For some reason, this neighborhood seemed very familiar to him. Levi ducked behind some garbage cans, feeling a bit silly to be sneaking around at night, but he wasn't the only one doing it, after all, was he? Granton was the last place on earth he would have thought to have dark secrets, but something was going on, and he had to find out what it was. The figure stepped onto a dark porch and began talking. Levi couldn't see who else was on the porch but heard a voice that he knew all too well.

"Did he see him?" the voice asked.

"No, he just went in to see if he was there," said the person that Levi guessed he'd been following.

"Did he go back to the Wilson house?"

"He was getting into his car when I left," the sneaking figure replied. Levi's skin began to crawl. It'd never occurred to him that someone could be listening to his conversations or following him around town.

"We need him out of Dorothy's house until we can find that medal. I don't want him to find it first. We are this close." Levi imagined wrinkled old fingers held up in a dainty pinching motion. That was Violet Beetle's voice. After hearing her talk in the coffee shop today, it had melded in his mind forever, but the other voice was one he couldn't place.

"I left Silas today for good, and I guess that's why he turned himself in. He was nothing without me, and Jerry will have his boys down here in no time to take care of him," the sneaking figure gloated.

Levi listened closely, trying to remember everything that was said. Silas must be in bigger trouble than he thought.

"Yes, I saw that you put in a call to New York today," Violet said.

The man must be Silas' driver. So, he left Silas today and was staying at Violet Beetle's house? That didn't make any sense.

"Well, it's been a long day. I think I'll head to bed. Good night," Violet said, finishing the conversation. Levi heard the wooden porch squeak and groan as she made her way into the house.

"G'night, Mom," the figure replied.

So *that* was it. Clayton and Violet had been following Silas for a long time. Clayton kept an eye on Silas, trying to figure out if he had any clue to where the medal was and Violet's odd behavior toward him in the coffee shop meant that she was following him to see what he knew. Their intentions were becoming clear. They were after the medal.

He had to tell someone this but didn't know who.

Levi wasn't sure if anyone would believe him anyway, because he had no proof.

He waited a few moments to make sure that both of them had gone into the house then took off at a sprint. Levi raced down the sidewalk, turned the corner, cut through the lot, and went back between the trees next to the jailhouse parking lot. He ran to his car and leaped into the driver's seat.

He needed to figure things out. A wave of information jumbled around in his head, but this much was clear; Clayton and Violet were after Grandma's house, the family treasure, and they wanted Silas dead.

*****

Abigail opened her eyes the next morning and rubbed her hand across her forehead. Her head ached, and she didn't want to move it. Gently, she leaned up in bed and began massaging the back of her neck. That helped the pain ease a little, and Abigail decided to try and push past it to begin her day. She quickly dressed and made her way downstairs, half expecting to be met by Levi to talk about what'd happened yesterday evening. When she came into the living room though, he was nowhere to be found. *Strange*, she thought to herself. In the kitchen, she saw her mom leaning over a bowl of cereal to take a bite.

"Morning," she announced. Her mother was still chewing but nodded a reply.

"Dad went to work early this morning and asked me to tell you to meet him there," Nancy explained after swallowing.

Abigail made herself a bowl of cereal as well. "Have you seen Levi this morning?" she asked her mother.

"Actually, no," Nancy said with a tone that told Abigail that she'd also expected to see him for breakfast. The two finished eating in silence as the room seemed to fill with concern over Levi's absence, but Abigail did her best to ignore it. She began to grab her things and was starting to leave when her mother stopped her.

"Abigail, I know you like Levi, but I want to tell you that I have a feeling about him that I'm not comfortable with," Nancy's eyes were filled with concern.

Abigail looked at her mother confusedly. "Mom, I thought you liked him, too. Why was he invited to stay here then?" she asked.

Nancy held up her hand. "No, that's not what I mean, Abby. I would just be careful until the business with Dorothy's house is sorted out," Nancy tried to explain. But that didn't make things any clearer to Abigail. Without asking anything further, she kissed her mother on the cheek and left.

Abigail couldn't help but think about Levi during her entire drive to the office. With his past and the present now, he seemed to come with a lot of emotional baggage and complicated relatives. Was this someone she was falling for? Her head told her that she really didn't want to get involved with a guy like that, but her heart was being reckless and stubborn.

Once she reached the office, Abigail decided that burying herself in her work was exactly what she needed after so much time off at home... with Levi around.

*****

Silas awoke in the all-too-familiar cell. This time, though, he wasn't anxious or worried, and he didn't feel the need to pace. Silas had accepted his fate and knew he deserved what was coming. He simply remained on the cot. The gray walls still filled him with sadness though, and he felt like there was something he'd left undone, but he wasn't sure what it was. He took slow, deep breaths, trying to relax so he could fall back asleep, but it was no use.

Down the hall, the squeak of a door opening informed him that someone was coming back to where he was.

Silas sat up and saw Levi walking toward him. He wasn't dreaming, was he? He had to be. Levi was the last person on earth that would come to see him.

"Levi, what are you doing here?" Silas asked. The expression on Levi's face was different from what Silas expected. He didn't look like he was there to kill him.

"I didn't believe them when they told me that you

turned yourself in," Levi said, stuffing his hands into his pockets.

"Well, as you can see, I did. I'm done running." A flicker in Levi's eyes revealed that his cousin knew what he was referring to. Silas wondered how he'd found out.

"Who is Clayton?" Levi demanded, taking a step toward Silas.

"That's none of your business. Besides, he is no longer part of this. He left town."

"Are you sure about that?" Levi replied.

Silas frowned at Levi and gave him a dismissive shrug.

"He's still in town, Silas, and they want both of us to lose Grandma's house so they can buy it," Levi quickly explained.

"Wait, who are *they*?" Silas asked. He'd only been in jail for a day and already felt like he'd missed so much.

"Clayton is staying with his mother. Her name is Violet Beetle. Apparently, she's been trying to steal our family treasure for a while now. Ulysses S. Grant gave his solid gold Medal of Honor to his sister, Virginia Corbin. Virginia Corbin was our great-great-grandmother," Levi blurted out in one long breath.

Silas was confused by all the information flying at him all at once but now realized that Levi had been holding details from him regarding the house. He wanted to get angry about it but realized that he would have done the same thing if their roles were reversed. Silas shook off the anger and tried to process everything Levi was telling him.

"You probably don't remember the Beetle," Levi continued, "but she used to live right by the park and terrorize the kids all the time."

Silas nodded in reply. "She took the basketball we were bouncing off the side of her house that one time," Silas reminded him.

Levi's eyes widened at the memory. "I forgot about that. You know, I think that was the only summer of you coming here that we got along," Levi said, directing his gaze at the floor.

Silas was growing a little nostalgic with the trip down memory lane and

was afraid that Levi was going to bring up more of the past but was glad when he didn't.

"I guess you could say that's the real reason I'm here," Levi went on.

"What do you mean?" Silas asked, even more confused by Levi's behavior.

"I never made it easy for you to be happy here. I may have even contributed to your current situation by treating you like the black sheep of the family when I really should've been there for you," Levi continued. Silas looked Levi in the eye, trying to determine his sincerity.

Silas turned away from Levi and faced the wall. Levi shouldn't be the one apologizing. So why was he?

"Levi, stop," Silas interrupted. "I should be the one apologizing to you for how I've treated you our whole lives. I've been a complete disappointment to everyone. My parents, our grandmother, and you." Silas suddenly felt a hand reach through the bars and tightly grip his shoulder.

"Why do you care about disappointing me?" A question Silas knew he would ask. So, Silas gave the answer that had been in his heart for a long time.

"Because I was jealous of what you had, and I knew I could never have it. You had so much love and a stable home and having lost parents that loved you had to be better than having parents who didn't care if you were around or not and fought all the time." Tears stung Silas' cheeks. He felt that he'd completely spilled his guts for the first time in his life. He had to trust someone to do that and Levi was all he had left.

"I've forgiven you. For everything," Levi said. Silas dropped his head. He didn't deserve Levi's forgiveness. He didn't even deserve to live at this point, but for some reason, his life was changing for the better.

"I don't feel like you did me wrong in any way, but if it helps, then I forgive you too," Silas replied, hoping he chose the right words.

"It does help. Thank you," Levi had tears streaming down his face as well. It felt strange to bond with Levi this way, but he was glad it happened.

"I only wish Grandma were here to see this. It was all she ever wanted for us. To be friends," Levi added.

"I wish I could apologize to her also," Silas felt the pain of regret a little stronger.

"She would be proud of you, Silas," Levi stated. The two stood to their feet and reached their arms through the bars. As they embraced each other, Silas felt a weight lift from his shoulders. Levi sighed, conveying to Silas that he felt the same thing.

"The only thing now is to face the family of that girl, Bella," Silas said, stepping out of Levi's hug. The feeling he had where he felt like something was left undone was gone now. Their grandmother could rest in peace; her boys had finally found a way to make things right between them.

A few feet away, a dark figure stood by the door. The cousins didn't notice him or sense the feeling of pride he felt upon seeing the two make up.

*Dorothy would have given anything to be here to see this happen*, Albert thought to himself.

Abigail sat behind her desk, wondering what it would take to get herself into work mode. She'd tried every method she knew when she arrived this morning, but nothing seemed to help. Levi filled her thoughts, and something was pulling at her to call him and apologize, but pulling in the other direction was her pride. Abigail considered simply filling out the reports that the house was Levi's due to Silas's criminal acts and that would be that. She wouldn't have to get involved anymore. Abigail repeated this to herself every time Levi's face appeared in her mind.

Part of her still wanted to help Levi finish solving the mystery of his family and find Grant's Medal of Honor, but if she didn't, she would read about it in the news soon enough. Levi had to be getting close, and with everything that had gone wrong for him, she was glad that something was about to go right.

Abigail closed her eyes tight and lifted her arms above her head in a big stretch. Maybe if she took a little break, she could clear her head and come back ready to work. She stood from her chair and took a few steps back from the desk, dropping to the floor in a squatting position to stretch her legs before she took her break. After standing back up, she grabbed her purse and started for the exit, but just as she was about to grab the handle, a knock vibrated the door and Abigail froze.

She wasn't expecting anyone, and the secretary hadn't let her know that anyone was waiting to talk with her. Was it Levi? Abigail opened the door, expecting to see his handsome face and icy blue eyes, but it wasn't him. Instead, there was a short round woman with frizzy gray hair and a yellow envelope in her hand.

"Ms. Beetle! What a surprise. I wasn't expecting a visit from you today," Abigail said, trying to look like she wasn't disappointed by the fact that it wasn't Levi at the door.

"I know," Violet replied coldly. Abigail was put off by her tone and instantly grew uncomfortable that Ms. Beetle was in her office. She placed her purse back on the chair where it had been just a few seconds ago and went back around her desk. Abigail gestured toward the chair on the other side of the big desk, and Ms. Beetle floated across the room and seated herself.

"What can I do for you, Ms. Beetle?" Abigail asked.

"I want the deed to the Corbin house," Violet stated, looking down her nose at Abigail. Abigail wasn't sure she'd heard her correctly at first but was sure that something was wrong with her.

*Did she miss her medicine or something?* Abigail's mind went in several different directions.

"Um, I can't do that. The house is currently owned by Dorothy Corbin's grandsons."

"No, it is not," Ms. Beetle replied, holding Abigail's gaze as if challenging her.

"What makes you say that?"

Ms. Beetle slapped the envelope down on the table. "I own it," she stated matter-of-factly.

Abigail grabbed the envelope and opened it. Glancing at the papers inside, she picked up the receiver to the phone that sat on the corner of her desk and called her dad, telling him to meet her in the office immediately. This wasn't something she wanted to handle alone.

\*\*\*\*\*

Levi sat in a chair in front of Silas' cell. The two of them had been swapping childhood stories for hours, and both were happier than they had been in a long time. Levi was starting to feel like he had a family again.

Glancing down at his watch, Levi realized that he'd been there talking with Silas for over three hours. That was the longest conversation they'd ever had. Suddenly, Albert stepped from the shadows and approached them, interrupting their conversation.

"Mr. Wilson! How long have you been standing there?" Levi asked as he stood to his feet.

"Long enough to know that your grandmother would be so happy and proud of you two," Albert replied with a grin.

Silas looked uncomfortable that Albert was there and fidgeted nervously.

"Levi, I got a call from Abigail. She needs both of us in her office ASAP," Albert said. Levi's stomach did a flip-flop. Did Abigail hate him that much? He knew he was a jerk, but this was a little much.

"But I still want to meet with both of you here after we find out what's going on with Abigail," Albert continued, switching his gaze from Levi to Silas and back again.

"That'll be easy. Not going anywhere," Silas joked, giving the bars on the cell door a firm shake.

Levi turned to Silas. "I'll be back as soon as I can. Then we can make some plans about ways to upgrade the house," he nodded to his cousin.

Silas replied with a half-smile as Levi followed Albert out the door.

*****

Abigail had a difficult time keeping Ms. Beetle entertained until her dad got there with Levi. As they sat alone in the office, Ms. Beetle made it a point to criticize almost every bit of decor that was in the room, from the curtains down to the carpet. After a course of judgments, though, she began talking about her work with the historical society and some of the discoveries that they had made in the state.

"Dorothy and I made some amazing discoveries back in the day," she finished. This direction of conversation finally sparked Abigail's attention.

"How well did you know Dorothy Corbin?" she asked.

"Oh, I've known her since college. She was always interested in the past, especially the Civil War. I don't know why. There's nothing significant about that war in my book. Now the Revolutionary War... We fought for our freedom! We took what was rightfully ours!" Ms. Beetle said, standing to her feet at attention, as if about to salute the wind. Her straight-backed posture told Abigail that she couldn't be nearly as old as she was making herself out to be. Something didn't feel right. Just then, Albert walked into the room with Levi at his heels.

"What seems to be the problem, Ms. Wilson?" Albert asked with the professional tone that he seemed to be able to turn on like a light switch.

Abigail took an inward sigh of relief at the sight of her father. As quickly and as professionally as she could, she explained the claims that Ms. Beetle was making and showed him the forms that were in the envelope. Abigail looked back at Levi to see his reaction to the news that his childhood home could be ripped away from him. He was frowning and shaking his head in disbelief. Abigail started to worry about what he might do.

"I'm sorry, Ms. Beetle, but this has to be a mistake. Grandma left the house to me and Silas. She wrote out this big—"

"Levi," Abigail cut him off and gave him a look that said to shut up. Levi didn't look happy.

"May I see you outside, Mr. Corbin?" she asked, tugging on his sleeve to convey that she meant business. He waited a moment then followed her. Abigail led him out to the front step where he'd brought her coffee just last week.

Levi spoke first. "What's going on? This is all wrong," he began.

Abigail held up her hands, this time letting him know that she was going to cut him off.

"Levi, I know this is messed up. I was the one that helped your grandmother prepare the will that I read to you and Silas, but until we can prove otherwise, the paperwork that she has in her possession is legal."

"I don't understand how this is legal," Levi stared at her, waiting for her to explain.

"Remember when I read the part of the will where it said that if you two don't work together then you get nothing?" she started.

Levi nodded.

"Apparently, she has been given full control of the house by the historical society that your grandmother was a part of. That's where the house would have gone if you two didn't want the house or if you failed to fulfill her dying wish," Abigail finished.

Levi shoved his hands in his pockets. "So, that is what she meant," he said, dropping his head.

"What do you mean? What who meant?" Abigail asked.

Levi told her of Clayton sneaking around in the dark the previous night and the fact that he was Ms. Beetle's son. He also told her how a "Jerry" in New York was involved and how they wanted both him and Silas out of the picture.

"Abigail, they want the medal," Levi finished. Abigail knew this, but more importantly knew that Levi would lose something that was a big part of who he was. Dorothy kept that house up to the best of her ability so that when the time came, her grandsons could do something amazing with it.

"Levi, there really isn't anything I can do at this point. Nothing major is going to happen until we can get this figured out," Abigail explained.

"Only her getting a key to the house. That's all she's after," Levi urged.

"Look, Levi, why don't we at least go over to their office tomorrow and talk to them about it. Maybe we can work something out. They may even let you keep searching for the medal."

"If we tell them about what we've found, there will be others looking for the medal. I need to find it first," Levi pointed out.

He stomped down the concrete stairs and walked off down the street. Tears began to roll down Abigail's cheeks. Did he think she was taking Ms. Beetle's side? She had to do things according to the law. If he lost the house for good, would he leave town? She didn't know if she would have the strength to watch him get back on the train.

*****

Silas looked out between the bars of his cell. His arms were folded through the bars, giving him a sense of being on the outside, at least partially. There wasn't much to look at in the jail. One gray splotch on the wall here, one black stain there. Silas contemplated them for a while to distract himself. How did those stains end up there? What caused them? The gray one looked as if it was some sort of spill that had darkened over time. Maybe someone had dropped a tray of food or a pot of soup or something and sent a splash up the wall? It wasn't very wide but rather tall, with the spill nearly reaching the ceiling. Silas would have hated being the person to make such an ugly mark and to always be reminded of it.

The black stain, on the other hand, was shaped like a sun that took up a corner of the room near the end of the hall. It was inside the last cell and looked as though someone had started a fire. As Silas looked closer, he could see that he had been right and that there were still bits of soot on the floor. A fire *had* broken out in the cell. How long ago did it happen? Silas would have to ask someone about that. At least the black stain wasn't as ugly as the other one. It looked almost beautiful.

Silas' mind then turned to the visit from Levi. He never would have guessed in a million years that they would've ever had a civil and pleasant conversation. It was as if Levi was a totally different person. It was then that Silas realized that he didn't really recognize himself either. He felt better. Lighter than he had in a long time. He and Levi had made amends and Levi promised that he would come back for a visit. He was thankful for something to look forward to.

The future was still gray from here, but Silas felt that he could face it with courage because he had friends and family.

Footsteps followed a door creaking open down the hall. Through it walked a uniformed figure that Silas had to squint his eyes to try and identify. He had not seen this officer before. He was a lean man with a bald head and a beard that trailed down the front of his shirt to his chest.

"Hey," Silas grunted. The officer tilted his head to the side and widened his stance. Silas knew he was attempting to look intimidating, but he didn't care. Rather, Silas wanted to know why he was acting this way.

"You know who I am?" the man asked Silas.

"No, but I know where you're from," Silas replied. He pulled his arms back into the cell.

"Jerry got a call and sent me," the officer said.

Silas had thought he had more time, but for this to

happen, Clayton must have turned him in. After everything they'd been through, too.

As the cold air blew down the street, Levi walked down the sidewalk back to where his car was parked at the jail. He had just experienced a breakthrough with Silas, connecting with him for the first time ever. Now, for the first time, Levi felt that their grandmother's legacy was finally something to be proud of. He had always thought that the legacy she left behind would be the rich history of brave men and women who lead difficult lives to protect their families and make a better future for their children.

That sounded just like Dorothy, after all. She'd sacrificed so much when she took him in, and Levi always had her love. Silas had her love as well, though he hadn't realized it back then. Levi's feelings and emotions had been building up inside of him since her funeral last week, and he knew that he hadn't cried for her the way she deserved. As Levi continued his walk, a tear trickled down his cheek, and the day seemed to get a little darker. He walked past a small, vacant lot with freshly mowed grass before stopping to look at it.

The lot was bordered by connecting streets on two sides and a tree line that stood guard along the other two sides. A group of small birds were pecking at the grass, looking for worms and bugs when a car horn blared, sending the birds into a flapping frenzy as the group glided into the sky. Levi watched them fly away, but his gaze was brought back down to the ground at the sound of chirping.

A single bird was fluttering and leaping, frantically trying to get off the ground so it could follow its friends, but something seemed to have it stuck. Levi walked over to the bird and grabbed it. Holding it still, he tilted it over to see what was preventing it from flying away. An old piece of red yarn was wrapped around its foot. Levi gently untangled the small creature and placed it back on the ground. The yarn must have somehow found its way here from the dumpster that sat nearby.

The bird looked up at him as if to say thanks, then took off like a speeding bullet. Levi watched it go for a few seconds. He knew how that bird felt and understood all too well how it felt to be abandoned by the people he loved. Levi had also had a few pieces of yarn holding him back from time to time. The difference between the bird and himself was that the bird flew once again without hesitation. Levi wanted to be that way as well, but he didn't feel like flying anymore.

His home was about to be taken away. Even if letting the historical society take ownership was the right thing to do, how was he supposed to find the strength to let it go and be ok with the fact that it was him that lost it? The Corbin family had been in that house for generations. Levi took in a deep breath and straightened his posture as he thought about the two Corbin brothers that fought to get to America for their families. Would they have just given up?

No, even when one of the brothers died, the other kept going until he found their home. Levi knew he couldn't just let the house go without a fight. He came from a long line of fighters and he was going to stick with tradition. There had to be something he could do. He would go with Abigail to the historical society, not to beg them to let him still have a say in what happened to the house, but to let them know that they were in for a fight.

Levi turned and started back down the sidewalk the way he'd come. It would take about an hour to get back to where his car was parked at the jail. He had ridden with Albert to the office to meet with Abigail and now he regretted it, but at least it gave him time to come up with a plan.

*****

Abigail felt like Ms. Beetle had taken up most of her day. The old woman had seemed a bit more upbeat than normal, which was strange in its own way. Her mind thought back to what Levi told her that he'd overheard. Could there really be some sort of scheme to get the house away from him and Silas? It would make sense based on the fact that finding General Grant's Medal of Honor would not only be a national treasure but a valuable one at that. The person who discovered it could make a fortune.

Although Abigail was glad to learn from her dad that Levi had forgiven Silas and made peace with him, she reminded herself that Silas was not a total victim of this situation like Levi was. A young girl was about to lose her life because of what Silas had done, and for that, he would have to face the consequences.

She locked her office door as she left, dropping her keys into her purse. Thinking about Levi and Silas had reminded her that she needed to go see Bella's parents and let them know that she was available if they needed anything.

Once Abigail stepped outside, a heavy breeze blew her hair right into her face and mouth. She spit the few rogue strands out of her mouth and climbed into her car. The sky had turned a sad gray as if the day had prepared itself for the tragedy that seemed to be striking everyone. Starting the engine, Abigail turned the car in the direction of the hospital.

She flipped through the stations on the radio, hoping to find a song that would lift her spirits, but didn't find anything. So, she rode in silence, thinking about the events of the past week. Abigail was emotionally and physically exhausted and wanted nothing more than to crawl into bed with a bucket of ice cream and cry her eyes out, but she couldn't. She had to reach out to Bella's family like she wished she had for Bella.

By the time she reached the hospital, tears were rolling down her face. If Abigail felt this responsible for what had happened, she could only imagine how Levi felt. Before she stepped out of her car to valet park, she paused for a moment and wiped her face clean of tear stains.

After entering the hospital, it took a few minutes for her to remember how to get back to Bella's room, but when she did, she saw a sight that she was sure would never leave her. A man and a woman sat in Bella's room with arms wrapped around one another. Their eyes were puffy and had dark circles under them, but along with the tears and exhaustion, there was something else in their eyes as well. A small glimmer of hope.

This confused Abigail, because she was sure that Levi had told her that the Rodríguezes would have to let their daughter go. Had something happened to change that? Bella was still lying in the same position she was when Abigail had last seen her, though the bruises on her face looked like they were starting to heal. She approached the open door and gave a gentle knock on the door-frame.

"Mr. and Mrs. Rodriguez?" Abigail asked gently. The couple looked up from one another's gazes and stood to their feet. She wanted to tell them to sit back down but started feeling awkward. Maybe she should have waited to come back with Levi.

"I'm Abigail Wilson. Levi Corbin's attorney," Abigail continued. "I met Bella a few times after she arrived in town, and I just wanted to come back and check on her again." Now she really wished Levi was here. Abigail couldn't remember ever feeling this insecure about herself before. What was happening?

Mr. Rodriguez approached her. Abigail suddenly had the urge to back away, but she fought it off. She didn't know what she was expecting him to do, but all he did was stick a hand out for her to shake. Abigail shook it awkwardly, wincing from his firm grip. His dark brown eyes were full of pain, and they were identical to Bella's eyes.

"I am Quinn Rodriguez, and this is my wife Mila," he explained to her.

"Pleased to meet you," Abigail stated, giving the woman a handshake as well.

"I just want to let you both know that I'm here if you need any legal help or need me to bring you anything or...." Abigail shrugged, not sure what to say to finish that sentence. Clearly, there wasn't anything she could do for them. The awkward tension of the situation made Abigail feel as if they were glaring at her when, in reality, both wore a welcoming smile. They didn't blame her or Levi for this, did they? If the Rodriguezes did decide to press charges against Silas for assault, Abigail wouldn't be allowed to go against her own father. Silas' would already be the most difficult case that their firm had ever handled.

She didn't know what she had been thinking of, offering her help like that.

"Please come and sit," Quinn gestured to the chair where he had been holding his wife just a few moments before. Abigail did as he asked. The two stood at the foot of the bed, staring at her, waiting for some further explanation for why she'd come.

"I can't even imagine what you two must be going through," Abigail burst out. Mila placed a hand on Quinn's shoulder.

"It's the hardest thing we've ever dealt with. Isabella is our only child," Mila whimpered. She wiped a tear from her eye and brushed back a jet-black twist of hair that fell into her face.

"My parents lost a child several years ago, my brother, leaving me their only living child. But even though he's gone, they say that they didn't really lose him, if you know what I mean."

The two dropped their gaze to the floor and Abigail continued, hoping to find some words of encouragement.

"I found that my faith helped me heal the most after I lost my little brother," Abigail offered.

That was when Quinn decided to surprise Abigail. "I am actually a minister in our hometown. I run a home missions church, and I am well aware of the faith that you are referring to," he said with a smile.

Abigail was more relieved than surprised. Most of her friends didn't go to church and she had a hard time explaining her faith to them and was sometimes embarrassed by it.

"We always have hope that God's will is perfect, even if it's not what we want at the time," Mila chimed in.

Abigail was glad to hear of their faith, but there was one thing that bothered her about the situation. Should she ask, or was it a bad time? She decided to go ahead and ask because it would help set the situation into perspective.

"I want to ask you both something that you may not want to answer, but it would really help the case if you were both open about it," Abigail pushed on.

The pair looked at her with a quizzical frown.

"Why did Bella run away?" she asked.

Quinn looked at Mila, and Abigail saw their hopeful, inspired expressions fade into something else. Abigail couldn't tell if it was shame, regret, or guilt. Mila decided to explain.

"I'm afraid that is our fault," she confessed. "From the time Bella was eleven, we pushed her very hard in school, telling her that her grades would be a path to the life she would like to have when she grew up. Bella began to feel like her grades defined her. When she had good grades, she was little-miss-sunshine, but when they were poor, she wore black. Bella told me one day that she didn't care about school anymore and wanted to quit." Mila burst into tears and buried her face in her husband's chest. Right on cue, Quinn took the story from there. He wrapped both his arms around his wife and continued.

"We told her it would shame us if she quit and that we could never show our faces in public again. Bella then told us that she already had quit. We were both outraged and said some things to her that we shouldn't have. So, as you may have now guessed, she didn't run away."

Abigail sat motionless for a moment. She knew the pressures from a parent, but nothing like what Bella had experienced. Abigail wanted to grab them and shake them and ask them why they would treat their own child that way, but instead she stayed in her seat.

"You kicked her out," Abigail murmured.

"This is our fault," Quinn nodded, letting a tear fall from his tightly closed eyes.

Abigail stood to her feet and went to where the couple stood at the foot of Bella's hospital bed. "This is something I don't normally do, but would it be alright if I prayed with you two?" She asked.

Quinn nodded and Abigail clasped both of their hands in hers and bowed her head. "Lord Jesus, we are devastated by what has happened to Bella. We know that we make some pretty horrible mistakes sometimes, but healing comes with forgiveness. We seek you first and thank you that we can come to you and ask without judgment. Please bring peace to us and help us through this difficult time. In your name we pray, Amen."

Abigail squeezed both their hands before letting go. They both smiled at her and thanked her.

"I have to go. I have a few appointments tomorrow, but if I have time, I'll stop by again," she said. They thanked her once again and Abigail left. She felt a huge ball of emotions sit heavily on her chest. Abigail was about ready to sit in a corner somewhere and cry her eyes out, but she felt that she'd better go check on Levi instead. He would need emotional support right now, too.

*****

Silas' arms were getting stiff and sore from being cuffed behind his back. This man that was impersonating an officer was going to take him off somewhere and kill him, he was sure of it. The fake officer had led him into the front of the building where two real officers stood talking. The man leading him out waved at the officers and they waved back with smiles spread across their faces as they approached.

"Hey, what's going on with the prisoner?" one officer asked the impersonator.

"He has a serious heart condition and is being moved to a jail with better medical care," his kidnapper explained.

"Our medical care here is just fine," the officer replied.

"Not according to the higher-ups. It's out of our hands," the impersonator said, holding up a form. "A family member filed for the transfer and the judge approved it."

Silas knew the form was forged, but the squeezing hand on his arm told him to keep quiet. Both officers looked at the document, asked to be given a copy upon filing, and then walked away. With the officers' curiosity apparently satisfied, Silas was led outside. He thought about making a run for it, but knew the gun on the man's hip would quickly stop him. There was no point in trying to escape if he'd just end up dead anyway.

The parking lot was full of cars this time of day, and a chilly gust of wind sent a shiver up Silas' spine. The sky was a dark gray, giving the impression that it would soon rain.

Silas glanced at the cars they were approaching, realizing that one of them looked familiar. As they came closer, it became clear; it was the rental car Levi had been driving. He must still be close by. Silas realized their destination was a squad car at the very end of the parking lot. Given the distance it was from the entrance, no one was going to realize what was going on until it was too late. Silas needed to think of something.

Suddenly, a voice came over the radio that hung at the officer's side. Silas couldn't make out what was being said, but it caused his kidnapper to pause for a moment before they stepped between two cars. With a hand in his back, the fake officer pushed Silas up against a nearby car, pressing him into the glass. It was Levi's rental. The man replied to the call on the radio with a few comments about being busy at the moment, and Silas could tell that he was having a difficult time coming up with things to say that wouldn't bring any attention to himself.

While the man was distracted, Silas began scribbling a message into the dirt on the top of Levi's car. Ideally, he would've used his nose for the job, but he knew it would leave dirt on the tip of his nose and that would give him away, so he decided to use his tongue.

He only had a few seconds to scrawl his message before the man pulled him up off the car and pushed him the rest of the way to their destination. Silas wanted to spit the taste of dirt out of his mouth, but that would've given him away too. So, he swallowed the taste instead, hoping he would never have to do that again.

Levi's legs began to tense up from walking so long. Since he'd come back to Granton, he'd been walking more than he had in years, and it showed just how out of shape he'd become. Finally, though, he could see the police station coming into view. After calming down, Levi had decided he would go back to Abigail's house to see if she or Albert had come up with some way to save his house from being taken away from him forever. As he approached his rental car Levi stepped onto the sidewalk, being that the sidewalk was about 5 inches thick, it allowed him to catch sight of some weird rub marks on the roof.

"What in the world?' he muttered to himself, turning his head sideways to see that some of the marks were letters. H, L P S I. Levi turned his head a bit more. Yes, that was definitely an E. HELP SI, it spelled out. Silas? That was the only "Si" he knew. Levi frowned and walked into the jail. Only one person was visible as he made his way inside. It was the same lady that was behind the huge desk the last time he asked if Silas was really here, and he wondered for a minute how she would react to the deja vu moment.

"Um, hello again. Can I ask if Silas Corbin is still here?" he said awkwardly. Levi didn't want to give her the impression that he didn't trust the police or that he was some sort of prankster, but just as he feared, she looked at him completely unamused.

"Look, someone wrote a message on my car that says 'help si,'" he explained, "and I just want to see if he's alright."

"Alright, but I'm gonna need to see some ID," the woman added flatly. Levi pulled his driver's license from his wallet and slid it across the desk to her.

The woman squinted at the little card and started typing on the computer sitting in front of her. She frowned at the bright screen just as she'd done before. This time, Levi decided to intervene. "I'd really appreciate it if you went back there and checked on him yourself, or at least allowed me to," Levi said, trying his best to mind his manners under the current circumstances.

"I don't have to. He was moved earlier today to another jail due to a heart condition," she told Levi.

"What? That's impossible. He doesn't have a heart condition!" Levi barked at her.

"There's an order on file that the judge moved him per the request of a family member," she explained.

Levi's anger turned to confusion. They had no other family members, at least that he knew of.

"Does it give the name of the family member that submitted the request?" Levi asked.

The woman scanned through the document, looking for a name. She then looked at him strangely. "The name says Levi Corbin."

"I never filed for any transfer," Levi declared.

"Yes sir, we'll get this figured out and get him back here," the lady officer said, picking up the phone. Levi feared that it was already too late for that.

\*\*\*\*\*

Abigail reached her house around dinner time, expecting to see Levi's car sitting in the driveway, but it wasn't there. So, she parked her car next to her dad's and hurried into the house. Abigail knew that Levi had a difficult day, and she was starting to worry that he would do something drastic.

"Mom?" Abigail called as she walked into the kitchen, but Nancy wasn't there. From the office, Abigail could hear her dad's voice, so she made her way over to it.

"Hey, Dad, where's Mom?" she asked casually, hearing a tiny bit of her teenaged-self asking the same question. Albert held up his hand, murmuring into the landline phone that was placed up to his ear.

"Yes, I'll be right there," he said, placing the phone down on the receiver. "That was the police," Albert told her before she could ask what was going on. "Silas seems to have vanished into thin air, and Levi is down at the station. Silas was taken by a man in a police uniform, but they haven't yet figured out who that man is or where he is from."

Abigail's chin nearly hit the floor. She couldn't believe what she just heard.

"Are they sure Silas didn't know the man and didn't plan this himself?" she asked.

"I wouldn't put it past him to try and escape," she finished to herself in a mutter.

"I really don't think that's what happened, but either way Levi shouldn't be down there by himself. It would really be easy for them to arrest him on suspicion, so I'm headed down there now," Albert said.

Abigail reverted to her original question, deciding that she would let her dad handle the current situation that Levi found himself in.

"Where's Mom?"

"She's over at the church helping the ladies plan the fall picnic for next weekend."

*That's right!* Abigail had totally forgotten about the fall picnic. She didn't really want to go over and rub shoulders with the ladies at the church right now but thought the planning might do her some good and help her take her mind off of things. Abigail followed her dad outside.

"Would you mind dropping me off by the church?" she asked him.

"Don't you want to come, too?" Albert asked.

"Not really. Plus I promised Mom I would stop by and help," Abigail replied. She didn't want to go into detail about wanting to keep her distance from Levi right now, nor did she want to go into detail about how she felt. For some reason, her response seemed to take him by surprise.

"Alright, but we need to hurry. I don't like this situation," Albert said.

Abigail knew he was concerned for Levi. He liked him, but Abigail suspected that had more to do with the promise he'd made to Dorothy than his opinion of Levi himself. As they drove along the familiar roads, Abigail decided to let herself think out loud.

"Did Levi tell you what he overheard at Ms. Beetle's house last night?" she asked.

Her dad shot her a look.

"No. Why was he eavesdropping on a conversation at Ms. Beetle's?"

"He seems to think that she and her son are after... some of the expensive antiques that are at Dorothy's house." Abigail breathed an inward sigh of relief. She'd promised not to tell anyone about the medal until Levi found it.

"Her son left town years ago, and no one has seen him since," her dad explained.

"Well, Levi is sure that he's back and that he's helping her, but he can't prove it," Abigail finished. The entire situation was unlike any case that Abigail had dealt with since she began practicing law. She hoped her dad would help her make sense of it all and say something to help her feel better, but he didn't. They were nearly at the church before Albert finally spoke up.

"Did Levi say anything else about Ms. Beetle's son?"

"Just that he is actually Clayton, Silas's driver," she replied, watching her father's expression change to one of total surprise. As the church parking lot came into view, Abigail waited for her father to slow the car down, but he seemed to be keeping his speed instead. She gripped the handle that was just above her head as they peeled into the parking lot. Her dad had called it the panic handle when she was learning to drive, and now she understood why.

They pulled into the parking lot so fast that Abigail feared they would hit something or someone. As they came to a screeching halt, her dad practically pushed her out of the car and then he sped off for the jail. It still didn't make any sense to her what was going on, but if anyone could take care of it, Albert Wilson could.

*****

Silas shifted his wrists, continuously trying to ease the pressure that the tight cuffs were causing. He could feel his skin tearing and burning from rubbing raw against his restraints. Silas had figured he would end up in some trunk to keep out of sight, but since this guy was disguised as a police officer, it didn't look suspicious at all to have someone sitting in the back of the car. Also, he was practically sitting on his hands, so the guy had no fear of him trying anything.

They drove past the outskirts of town and turned onto the highway. Normally in this situation, Silas would be smart enough to be quiet, hoping to avoid making the person restraining him angry. But he didn't need to worry about making his captor angry this time because he knew the man was going to kill him anyway. Silas had no idea how he could get out of this situation anymore.

"Where are you taking me?" he finally asked.

"You'll see," was all he got in reply.

"Look, I know you're going to kill me. It's not like I'm gonna be able to tell anyone your plans afterwards," Silas shot back. The man laughed so hard that the car gently swerved, and Silas could see his long beard bounce up and down.

"I'm not going to kill you. I'm just the delivery guy," the man said. Silas frowned at the remark.

"You're going back to Jerry's, so get comfortable. We've got a long trip ahead of us," his captor continued.

Silas didn't reply. It wasn't what he had expected from Jerry, but maybe there was still some hope that he could survive this. There was, however, no way for him to get comfortable with the handcuffs still on.

*****

Levi sat anxiously in a bright room at a table with an

empty chair on the other side. They had questioned him more times than he could count about whether he knew the man that took Silas or if he knew anything else that would help them track him down. Levi had shown them the writing on the top of his car and told them that it was then that he knew something was wrong.

"What some people will do for family," one officer said to another, purposely letting Levi hear him.

"Look, until the last twenty-four hours, I didn't care what happened to Silas, but now he's in trouble and something needs to be done about it," Levi felt like screaming at the officers.

The officers asked him once more if he knew anything, and once more, he told them no. It seemed pretty clear that they suspected him of being involved and were fishing for any shred of proof. Finally, the officers stood to their feet and left him in that room alone. Levi had remained in the interrogation room for the last hour with nothing but time to think, and he didn't like it. The more he thought about his current situation, the more he realized that he wasn't the good person he'd always thought himself to be.

Without warning, the door swung open and an officer came back into the room with Albert in tow.

"Well, it looks like you are free to go," the officer said.

Levi had never been happier to see Albert. He always managed to show up at just the right time.

"We will put an APB out on Silas and the guy who

took him and get them both back here," the officer promised.

"Thank you," Levi replied. He wanted to give the officer a few more choice words, but he thought it best not to.

Levi walked to his rental car, wanting to drive out of Granton and never come back. Everything had been going just fine until this morning, and now it was all chaos once again. He gave a glance to the message that Silas had left for him before climbing into the car and starting it up. As he pulled out of the tiny police parking lot, Levi tried to imagine where Silas could be right now and what he could be dealing with, but that only caused him to grow angry and anxious. So, he pushed it from his mind and decided that it was best to leave it in the hands of the police.

What he could focus on now was finding Grant's medal. It had to be somewhere in the house, and Levi needed to find it before anything else happened. As he turned down the side road that led to the house, he decided that he wouldn't leave there again until he found it, no matter what happened. If Levi was really going to lose the house to the Granton Historical Society, he at least wanted the item that his grandmother treasured most.

When he arrived, Levi parked the car behind the house so it wouldn't be seen from the road; he didn't want anyone interfering or trying to stop him because of some legal technicality. He went in the back door and pushed his way past the fire-damaged door jamb. The stairs were badly burned, but Levi gently maneuvered his way up them in just a few minutes. Once he got to the room that he had been sleeping in just a few days ago, he set the duffle bag he'd brought with him on the floor.

Levi pulled out the book that he'd discovered in Grandma's room the day Abigail kissed him and stared at the cover, thinking about how close they had become since he'd first arrived in town. "No," he shook his head. He needed to focus. Running his fingers over the title, Levi took a deep breath.

If this really was *The Map* in more than just name, then he was going to figure out what the clues inside meant. He opened to the back inside cover, where the diagram of the second floor was. The number fourteen clue seemed to almost flash at him as if it was trying to tell him what it meant. Levi knew he had to be close, he could almost taste it.

The number was written just above the guest bedroom. Maybe that was the clue? Levi went down the hallway to the guest room that was right across from the entrance to the attic. Entering the room, he sat down on the bed and began to look around.

This room still looked exactly the same as it had when he had lived here. A twin-sized bed sat against the right wall with its lacy, white bedspread under a sheer canopy. Most of the furniture in the room was white, including the dressers, and a mannequin dressed in a beautiful white gown stood in the corner, suggesting that, at some point, this was a woman's room. There weren't any bookshelves here, though, which puzzled Levi. Every other clue that he had found had been in a book. So where could the next one be? After looking closely at every piece of furniture and picture on the wall, Levi sat back down on the bed in defeat, looking at the diagram once again.

He ran his finger over the image of the room he was in absentmindedly. His finger brushed against something, and he paused. There was dirt or mud on the page that lifted up just a tiny bit, like a bump. Taking his fingernail, Levi gently tried to scratch the hard substance off, and when he did, a small passageway on the diagram was revealed. It seemed to lead to a tiny room behind the closet.

"The fourteenth room," he said out loud, sending an echo through the house. It all made sense now. *That* was why Grandma had tried to memorize the numbered rooms in her head, so she wouldn't forget where the medal was hidden. Levi hurried over to the closet, almost unable to control his excitement. He pushed aside an old box that was full of garments. On the wooden back wall of the closet was a beautiful number fourteen, elegantly written with what seemed to be plaster.

It was painted white along with the rest of the wall to make it difficult to see. Levi began banging on the wall, hoping there was a button or something that would open. He didn't want to break it down with a sledgehammer, but he would if he had to. Luckily, there was a button in the top corner that sent the back wall of the closet swinging open when he hit it with his fist.

The passageway that opened up was narrow, and Levi had to turn sideways to get through it. He almost felt like Lucy Pevensie about to step into Narnia. Levi slowly walked down the small hallway, feeling amazed as the room opened up to reveal a good-sized room filled floor to ceiling with books.

"A secret library," he muttered to himself. "Room fourteen." Darkness filled the room, and a thick layer of dust covered the books and shelves, obscuring any titles or names. Levi picked up one of the books, sending a cloud of dust hovering in the room. He sneezed and decided to leave the books alone for now, until he could at least bring in a vacuum. As he walked around the library, more dust seemed to kick up into the air, as if in protest of his presence. A small window sat in the bottom corner of the room with a clear view of the front porch. Opposite the tiny window in another corner was a big box with a small eagle perched upon two large scrolls.

"That must be it!" Levi yelled, feeling as if he was

about to burst through the ceiling with excitement. He walked to the box and opened the lid gently. A beautiful gold medal lay snug on a red velvet pillow. This was such a big moment for Levi that he had to choke back tears. This treasure, his grandma's treasure, had been a huge part of his life, even before he knew what it was. Levi wished that Grandma could be here; he had so many questions that he wished he could ask her. Why did she keep such an amazing family secret hidden? Did she know about the secret library? About this room? Or did she just memorize the clues like she was told to by her family?

*This may give me the leverage I need to get the house back*, Levi thought. Gently he picked up the box, which was a bit heavier than he expected, and took it back through the narrow closet doorway. He would take this to the Wilsons, where it would be safe until they could figure out what was best to do with it. But just as he pushed his way out of the crowded closet, Levi noticed he wasn't alone anymore.

Clayton and Ms. Beetle sat on the white twin bed as if they had been waiting for him to bring the medal out to them. Clayton lifted up his arm, revealing a pistol at the end. A greedy grin spread over his face. Ms. Beetle followed suit, pulling a tiny derringer pistol out of her purse.

"Thank you for bringing that to me. You have no idea how long I've been searching for it," Ms. Beetle said with a sinister grin.

Abigail sat in a group of about ten or twelve women, most of whom she knew very well. The group was gathered in the sanctuary of the church, whispering and chattering amongst themselves. Up behind the pulpit stood Margret Steel, with her hands on her hips and her brow furrowed. She had been the pastor's wife for twenty years, was a bit of a control freak, and planning the fall picnic was one of her favorite things to do.

Abigail sat next to her mother at the end of the long row. She always went with her mother to these things, even though Nancy would often get preoccupied talking and making plans with Sharon Brandon, leaving Abigail to her thoughts. Although Abigail never fit in too well with these women, she loved and respected them. For years, Nancy and Sharon had been a team in the baking competition and were undefeated. It was just one of the many traditions in Granton that Abigail loved, and with so much happening lately that shook her world, she was happy to have something familiar and wholesome.

As Margret began assigning tasks to different ladies that were present, each one began writing down notes about what dishes they were going to bring and any details that they could add to make their dishes more special. Mrs. Steel continued rattling off other ideas and plans that she hoped would "change things up a bit" at this year's picnic. Amidst the chaos, Abigail began to wonder if Mrs. Rodriguez did this sort of thing in their church. Did she ever lead a group of people, or take over a church project in place of her husband? She didn't seem like the leading type to Abigail, but the thought of Mrs. Rodriguez's tired face and sad brown eyes gave Abigail an idea. She gave her mother a nudge with her elbow.

"What?" Nancy replied, keeping her gaze on Margret.

"Would you like to go with me this afternoon to invite the Rodriguezes to the picnic?"

"Who?"

"The parents of the girl who was attacked," Abigail whispered. She was surprised that her mother hadn't heard all about it from someone in town.

"Sure, that's a great idea," Nancy replied, still not looking at her. Abigail wasn't really sure she was listening, so she tried to come up with a compelling reason as to why the couple should leave their dying daughter for the afternoon. She doubted they would accept the invitation, but she wanted to make the offer as a simple gesture of kindness.

It wasn't long before the group of women stood to their feet, almost in unison, and herded themselves to the kitchen area that was located in the basement of the church. The kitchen would have to be cleaned and prepared for the massive amount of food that was going to be brought. There was a cafeteria-style window on either side of the room; one that led to an indoor dining area where round, cherrywood tables with six or seven chairs around each one sat that were donated by Sharon's husband several years ago. The other opened to an outdoor dining area with several picnic tables. A huge oak tree stood on each corner of the picnic area, and a jungle gym was set up off to the side for the kids.

Margret opened the window to the outdoor eating area and began wiping the metal countertop down. Abigail helped some of the other ladies clear leaves and debris from the tables and sweep the concrete floor. She hurried through her task as fast as she could, hoping to grab her mom and be off for the hospital while it was still early. Little did she know, it would be another hour and a half before Abigail would be sitting in the car with her mother. When the time finally did come for them to leave, Abigail tried to plan the conversation in her mind.

"This was a great idea, inviting them," Nancy exclaimed, interrupting Abigail's deepening thoughts. "Your father will be proud."

Abigail smiled at the compliment. During the entire

trip to the hospital, Nancy talked about some ideas she had for the baking competition and how she and Sharon were going to "up their game." Abigail tried to find the words to tell her mom that she was looking for a tactful way to invite the Rodriguezes to the picnic but never seemed to be able to find a great spot to interrupt. She didn't know anything about them and wasn't sure what would be considered crossing a line, but the only way to find out was to try and see what happened.

When they reached the hospital, Abigail pulled to the front entrance and allowed the valet to park her car, which wasn't something she normally liked to do, but she was in a hurry. The two women walked inside and down the hallway to the elevator, following the same path that Abigail had taken the last time she was here.

When they reached the ICU, there sat the Rodríguezes' holding each other's hands. Abigail could see that they still had some hope left.

"Hello again," Abigail quietly announced. The couple stood and greeted her.

"This is my mother, Nancy Wilson," she said with a smile. Nancy shook hands with them both and told them that she was happy to meet them and expressed her sympathy over their daughter's health. After a few moments of introductions and small talk, Abigail thought she'd better explain why they were there.

"My mother and I were at a planning event at our church this afternoon. Our church is planning a fall picnic for next weekend, and we would love for you to come if you are still in town," she offered. Abigail cringed inwardly, regretting her choice of words.

The couple looked at each other, unsure of how to reply. "Can we get back to you about that?" Quinn asked.

"Oh, yeah, definitely. I just wanted to invite you both and let you know that our church is praying for Bella," Abigail replied. She felt just like her mother saying that.

Nancy began explaining the list of events that took place at the picnic and embellished on all the wonderful things to eat that would be there. Abigail tried not to get embarrassed by her mother's enthusiasm for the baking competition, but couldn't help looking away, hoping she would stop. She glanced at the corner of the room, but a slight movement caught her eye. Was she crazy, or did Bella just blink? She stared at Bella's face for a few more seconds. No, it couldn't have been. It was wishful thinking making her see things, but still... Abigail continued staring at Bella's face, just long enough to see Bella's eyes open and look directly at her.

---

Levi stood still, too shocked to move a muscle. Violet and Clayton were sitting comfortably on the beautiful bed as if they belonged there. Knowing that they had been after the medal for so long, and that they were the reason that Silas had been taken off to god-knows-where, Levi realized he should have been more careful. The excitement over figuring out his grandmother's final mystery had pushed him to be rash and reckless, and now all he could do was grip the box tightly while racking his brain to figure out the best way to get out of here.

"You have no idea what I've been through to get that," Ms. Beetle exclaimed with a sigh of satisfaction. She tapped her son's leg with her gun, sending him to his feet. Clayton walked over to Levi and jerked the box from his hands. Levi felt a wave of burning anger move throughout his body, and it was all he could do to not leap at both of them in an attempt to strangle the life from their bodies. He had lost that battle and was about to leap when Ms. Beetle continued speaking.

"I've been trying to get my hands on this house for years. I offered Dorothy way more money than it's worth and even joined the historical society, hoping to learn any information about the medal. I'd hoped many times that she would bring some of her books for the group to analyze, but she never did. She was very protective of this place and her things," she explained.

As Violet continued to ramble about her genius plan, Clayton tapped her arm. "Mom,

stop talking or we're gonna have to kill him," he snapped at her.

"Hush, Clayton. That was the plan all along. He still technically owns the house after all. I'll torch the building myself this time, and the historical society, being the next owners of the house if they didn't follow Dorothy's will, can receive the insurance money. When they do, who do you think the treasurer in charge of that money will be?" Ms. Beetle placed her hand on her chest as if her plans were honorable.

Levi listened closely, trying to remember every detail just in case he made it out alive. If he did make it out, it would be all too easy to prosecute because of Ms. Beetle's uncontrollable desire to hear her own voice.

"So, are you going to kill me before you torch the house or after?" Levi asked, hoping to keep her talking.

"I haven't decided yet," she replied. "It's your own

fault, though. When I heard the details about Dorothy's will, I sent Clayton to track Silas down. It was so easy to drive him mad with money troubles, and it would have been easy to take the house after Dorothy passed, too, but before I could get the paperwork together, you had to get wise and figure out the clues she left. So, you see? It's your fault we'll be killing you," Violet smirked again.

Ms. Beetle stood to her feet and began walking toward Levi with the gun still pointed at his chest. He tensed, thinking she was about to pull the trigger, but she kept coming closer; so close that Levi was forced to take a few steps back. Violet kept advancing towards him, and he kept walking backward until he found himself back in the dusty medal room. Ms. Beetle stuck her head through the small closet into the room and stared at him for a moment.

"You won't make it out this time," she announced, smiling. Violet stepped back into the bedroom and the secret wall slammed closed, trapping him inside.

Levi figured there had to be a way to open it from this side but had no idea where to even begin looking. So, instead, he began searching the room for something that could break through the wall. There was an old bed warmer in the corner, and he considered using that but decided not to, figuring it wouldn't be strong enough. If only he had an axe or something. He turned and ran to the small window that overlooked the front driveway and rose garden. The window was shaped like a diamond and was about waist high to him. It was then that Levi began to smell smoke, and he saw plumes of it rising above the roof.

*That fire spread way too fast. They must've used gasoline.* Levi continued looking out the tiny window, praying someone would drive by and see the house on fire.

"I really didn't want to die like this. If you help me out of here, I promise I won't let this be the end of my family's legacy," Levi prayed. Levi could now smell the gasoline coming from the bedroom, confirming his suspicion. He pulled his shirt over his mouth and nose to avoid breathing the fumes.

*How much gasoline could they have possibly used?*

Levi heard movement on the other side of the secret doorway; they must've started the fire in the spare bedroom to ensure he couldn't escape. He saw more smoke coming from under the door, slowly seeping into the room. Levi quickly took off the flannel, button-up shirt he was wearing and stuffed it under the door to clog the gap. That would stop the smoke from coming in for a while, but he didn't have much time before the fire would completely eat the door away.

He thought about his cell phone that was absent-mindedly placed on the kitchen counter; Levi hadn't wanted anything to disturb him while he searched for the medal. He never would have imagined what that simple action would cost him, and he promised himself that if he made it out of here alive, he would never have his cell phone more than a few feet away from him again.

Levi's eyes began to water, so he closed them, expecting the smell of smoke and gasoline to make him pass out. If this was how he was going to go, Levi at least wanted it to be peaceful. He wanted to pass away thinking of the people that he loved: his family and his friends. Levi thought about all the wonderful things his grandmother had done for him since he first came to live with her. The effect she'd had on this town and on Silas' life, even when he tried his best to ignore it.

He hoped that the police would find Silas so he could take the property and do something special to remember the Corbin name. If the house survived at all, anyway; it would be gone within a few short hours unless someone got here soon. Just as Levi started sliding to the floor so he wouldn't fall and hit his head, he heard a door slam. He wasn't sure what it was but knew that it didn't come from the bedroom. Instead, it seemed to come from just outside of the small window. Levi got to his knees and peered through it. Two police officers ran across the garden. Suddenly he saw Clayton appear from the house as one of the officers took off after him on foot.

The other officer led Ms. Beetle out of the house in handcuffs. This was it! Rescue! Levi had to let them know he was here. He began beating on the glass with his fists and yelling at the top of his lungs, but they didn't seem to hear him. Just as the officers disappeared from his view, he saw Albert run across the lawn and into the house. For a moment, Levi filled with hope, but those hopes tempered themselves when he realized that Albert had no idea how to get to him. He would be dead before he could find Levi. He scanned the floor looking for something that would help him get their attention. Something that would help him break the window. He picked up the antique bed warmer that was leaning against the wall and discovered an old nail that was laying on the floor near it. Levi took them both and struck the window with the nail. The glass shattered, and Levi began banging the nail against the brass part. He yelled as loud as he could until Albert ran out of the house and looked up at the window.

"The spare bedroom at the end of the hall! There's a secret door inside the closet!" he called down to him. Without a word, Albert ran back into the house. Levi ran back over to the secret door. He could feel the heat coming through the wall as it grew hotter. Levi wondered how bad the fire was in that room but imagined it would only be getting worse. Was the closet blocked by flames? Would Albert be able to even reach him? Levi picked up the shirt that was blocking the smoke from coming under the door and wrapped his hand with it. He started beating on the door, still feeling the heat of the flames through the shirt. He knew the door was getting hotter by the second.

To his relief, the old secret door was slowly being pried open. Levi could see the edge of a crowbar sliding into the door jamb further and further until the door popped open. He quickly squeezed through the narrow passage, past Albert and ran out. The ceiling and part of one of the walls were wrapped in flames, but there was no time to worry about that. Levi ran down the hallway and down the previously burned stairs with Albert at his heels. The steps shook and moaned under his weight, and he was ready to leap off at any sign of them collapsing, but they were both able to make it to the bottom without an issue. Levi's lungs burned, and he desperately needed fresh air.

When he finally made it outside, he took a deep breath and choked a few times as the smoke began to clear from his lungs. Albert came up behind him and started patting him firmly on the back.

"The fire department will be here soon with an ambulance. You're gonna be alright. Just breathe," he said. Levi could hear that Albert was having a hard time catching his breath, too, but he wasn't in the house nearly as long, so Levi hoped he was alright. Albert helped Levi sit crossed-legged on the ground and continued coaching him to take deep breaths. His lungs continued to burn with each breath, and he felt like they were being torn into shreds, but Levi kept breathing.

Ten minutes later, a team of paramedics helped Levi to his feet and onto a narrow gurney. He tried to tell them to wait, but all that came out were gasps. Levi smacked one of them on the arm as they placed an oxygen mask over his nose and mouth. He leaned up off the gurney and pushed the mask off his mouth.

"Albert!" he wheezed. Albert turned from where the

police had Ms. Beetle and Clayton sitting on the ground and hurried over to him. Levi wanted to thank him and ask him how he'd known where he was and that he needed help, but his voice didn't allow it. Instead, he blurted out, "Medal!"

Albert grabbed his hand. "I'll see to it that it gets back to you as soon as possible," Albert promised. Levi gave his hand a squeeze. He hadn't had a father figure in a very long time, but he was glad for a true friend. Levi had learned so much from him since he'd come to this town, and he hoped to learn a lot more from him in the future. As the ambulance drove away from the house, Levi swore that he would do something to repay the man that saved his life.

# EPILOGUE

Albert leaned against the oak tree at the edge of the church's picnic area. Everyone invited had seemed to show up. There was music and laugher, and he could see Nancy hugging her friend Sharon with a blue ribbon clasped tightly in her hand. Levi could be found where he'd been for the last three weeks, right by Abigail's side. His daughter hadn't been so happy in years, and his heart wanted to burst at the sight. Dorothy's house had taken a lot of damage from the fire, but Levi had decided to rebuild it exactly as it was. Before that, though, he had decided to move here to Granton permanently. He was home to stay.

Albert had noticed a massive change in him since the first day he'd arrived, and it was too bad Dorothy wasn't here to see how his life had been changed by the legacy she'd left behind. Not only the family legacy but the legacy that helped Levi forgive Silas and put the past behind them.

Not much had happened in the last three weeks since Ms. Beetle and her son Clayton went to jail. The police were able to get them to spill the information on where Silas was being taken, and he was found in West Virginia at a rest stop. Silas would stand trial for the assault charge filed against him by the parents of Bella Rodriguez, but his life was finally headed in the right direction again. Abigail talked of nothing but the amazing recovery Bella was making all week. The doctors said that it would take some time, but she should make a full recovery, which was a miracle in itself.

Albert took a drink of the lemonade that he held in his hand. He wasn't much for parties but liked to at least show his face. Honestly, he mostly attended for Nancy's sake. Albert tipped up the cup to finish that last few sips, then worked his way over to where Levi and Abigail were standing.

"Yeah, I was thinking of turning the house into a museum," he overheard Levi say.

"That's an excellent idea," Abigail replied, enthusiastically.

"What are you guys talking about?" Albert jumped in. Levi and Abigail turned toward Albert to better include him in their conversation.

"Levi was just telling me how he was going to restore Dorothy's house and turn it into a museum," Abigail explained.

"Dorothy had so many books, documents and antiques from her family and the local area. I think that's an excellent idea," Albert grinned.

"Of course, it'll take some time for me to go through it, and I'll have to get some funding to get the museum opened," Levi reasoned. Albert began rubbing his beard in thought.

"Would you accept help from the Granton Historical Society?" Albert suggested.

"Yes! Now that I know they weren't really after my house and all the trouble was from the Beetle." The three nodded in agreement.

"Well, I have some work to do. I think I will head home now." After saying goodbye to the two that were sure to become a couple soon, Albert grew worried. Dorothy passed away before she was able to share with him where she'd hidden the diary. If Levi planned to go through everything, he would surely discover the secret that he and Dorothy were commissioned to keep. Albert remembered how clever Dorothy was. Maybe Levi wouldn't find it. There wasn't anyone else looking for the diary, at least he hoped not. Albert climbed into his car and pulled the seatbelt over his lap. As he grabbed the steering wheel, he noticed a note taped to it.

"We need to talk," it read.

### THE END?

# AUTHORS NOTE

---

This book has been on my heart for quite some time. I took an interest in the American Civil war a few years back, during my sophomore year of college. I toyed with the idea of the discovery of relics and the excitement and romance that comes with it. That was when Levi Corbin was born. There are many houses in my home-town that are similar to the Granton house. They have seen more than a century and have been home to more than three generations. It brings me almost a feeling of comfort to see the houses turned into a Bed and break-fast, or a museum, or simply kept up for tours. I am so thankful to everyone who helped me make this book a reality. And thank you for your curiosity. You now know the secret of the 14th room.

**Rebecca Hemlock** has been writing stories for many years and enjoys reading, painting and spending time with her family. Her favorite times to write are early in the morning when the sun is coming up and at sunset. She has worked as a freelance journalist for 4 years and is a member of Sisters in Crime and American Christian Fiction Writers. Rebecca has earned a degree in English and an Appalachian Studies certificate in Creative Writing. Rebecca lives in Eastern Kentucky with her husband and two children.

LOOK FOR BOOK TWO OF THE
GRANTON HOUSE SERIES IN
AUGUST OF 2021

**The Secret Diary of Deadly Deception**

Here's a sneak peek

Silas Corbin sat handcuffed in the back seat of a police car as the engine stopped. The uniformed figure sitting in the front seat was anything but a police officer. Silas had no idea how he was going to get out of this situation, nor did he expect anyone to be looking for him. He didn't think anyone would understand, nor would they find the message he left behind asking for help, but that was his only chance of getting out of this situation alive. Silas knew that the driver would try to put as much distance between them and Granton, Tennessee, as possible. They had made it as far as West Virginia when Silas thought of a way to get him to stop. If they stopped for a while, Silas would have a better opportunity to make his move.

His only idea was to beg to get out and relieve himself. After hours of begging, the man in the front finally gave in and pulled into a highway rest stop. He climbed out of the car and helped Silas to his feet and began taking off the cuffs.

"Don't be stupid, okay? In and out. Got it?" The bald, bearded man muttered as he took the handcuffs off of him and grabbed his arm, squeezing it for an answer.

"Okay! I got it!" Silas replied, holding up his other hand as if swearing. His captor reached into the car to grab the belt that held his gun. As Silas stood waiting, a family in a minivan pulled into the parking spot next to them, looking at Silas as if he was some hideous monster. He knew he used to be, but that wasn't him anymore. He saw the man in the driver's seat say something to his family and Silas knew he told them not to get out of the car yet.

"Ok, let's go," said the man as he tapped Silas on the back, urging him forward. Silas had hoped this guy would leave the gun in the car so as not to draw attention to them, but he didn't seem to be worried about that. The police uniform seemed to shield them from any suspicious activity. Silas had to mentally give kudos to the man for thinking up a genius disguise. They entered the main building where the restrooms were located.

"You have 5 minutes," The fake officer stated.

"Thanks a heap," Silas replied sarcastically before disappearing inside. The first thing he did as he entered the restroom was look for windows. He quickly ruled out that idea because the windows were about ten feet in the air and so small that he wasn't even going to try to fit through it. There was a fire exit located in the back of the room, but he knew that the alarm would immediately go off, alerting the entire building of his escape. He wouldn't have time to make it very far before being caught again. His chances of escape looked bleak at this point.

SIGN UP FOR REBECCA'S
NEWSLETTER. KEEP UP TO DATE
ON BOOK RELEASES AND
EVENTS.

*rebeccahemlock.com*